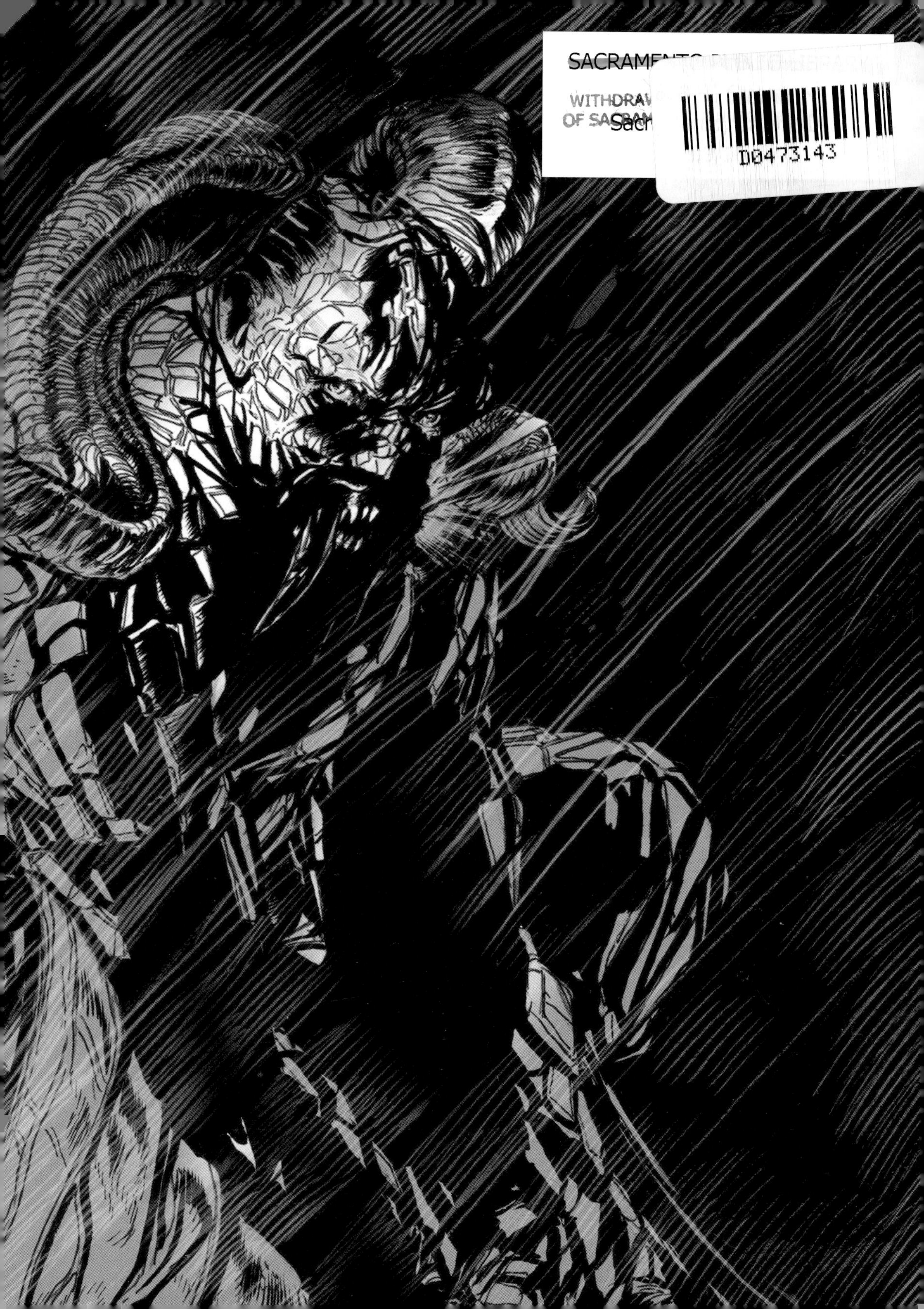

To my grandson, David Stemple, who knows Edinburgh well and loves graphic novels —JY

For Karrin and Big John, who loved the Auld Toun almost as much as we did —AS

This book is dedicated to the greatest parents in the world, Mark and Lisa Zangara, who are loving and always supportive of my drawing habits. Thank you for everything. —OZ

Story by Jane Yolen and Adam Stemple
Illustrations by Orion Zangara
Lettering by Bill Hauser

Graphic Universe™
A division of Lerner Publishing Group, Inc.
241 First Avenue North
Minneapolis, MN 55401 USA

For reading levels and more information, look up this title at www.lernerbooks.com.

Main body text set in CCWildWords 7/8. Typeface provided by Comicraft.

Library of Congress Cataloging-in-Publication Data

Names: Yolen, Jane. | Stemple, Adam. | Zangara, Orion, illustrator.
Title: Stone cold / by Jane Yolen and Adam Stemple ; Illustrated by Orion Zangara.
Description: Minneapolis : Graphic Universe, [2015] | Series: The Stone Man mysteries ; #1 |
    Summary: Silex is a talking gargoyle on a cathedral in Scotland who moonlights as a
    detective, assisted by a team of Scottish street urchins who do the grunt work.
Identifiers: LCCN 2014009423 | ISBN 9781467741965 (lib. bdg. : alk. paper) | ISBN 9781512411553
    (pbk.) | ISBN 9781512409031 (eb pdf)
Subjects: LCSH: Graphic novels. | CYAC: Graphic novels. | Gargoyles—Fiction. | Supernatural—
    Fiction. | Mystery and detective stories. | Scotland—Fiction.
Classification: LCC PZ7.7.Y65 St 2015 | DDC 741.5/973—dc23

LC record available at http://lccn.loc.gov/2014009423

Manufactured in the United States of America
1-36193-16977-3/2/2016

THE STONE MAN MYSTERIES

BOOK ONE

JANE YOLEN AND **ADAM STEMPLE**

ILLUSTRATED BY **ORION ZANGARA**

GRAPHIC UNIVERSE™ • MINNEAPOLIS

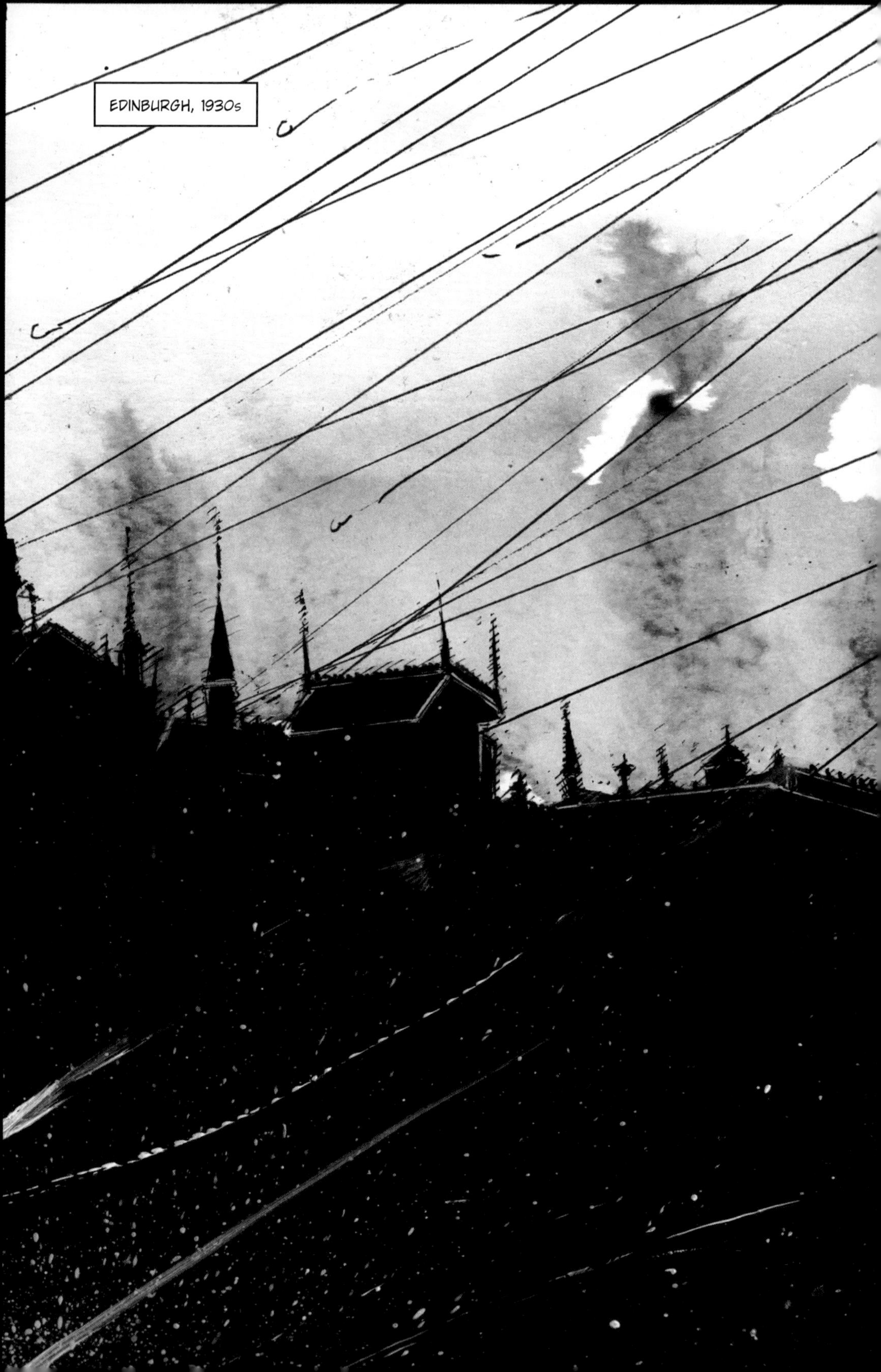
EDINBURGH, 1930s

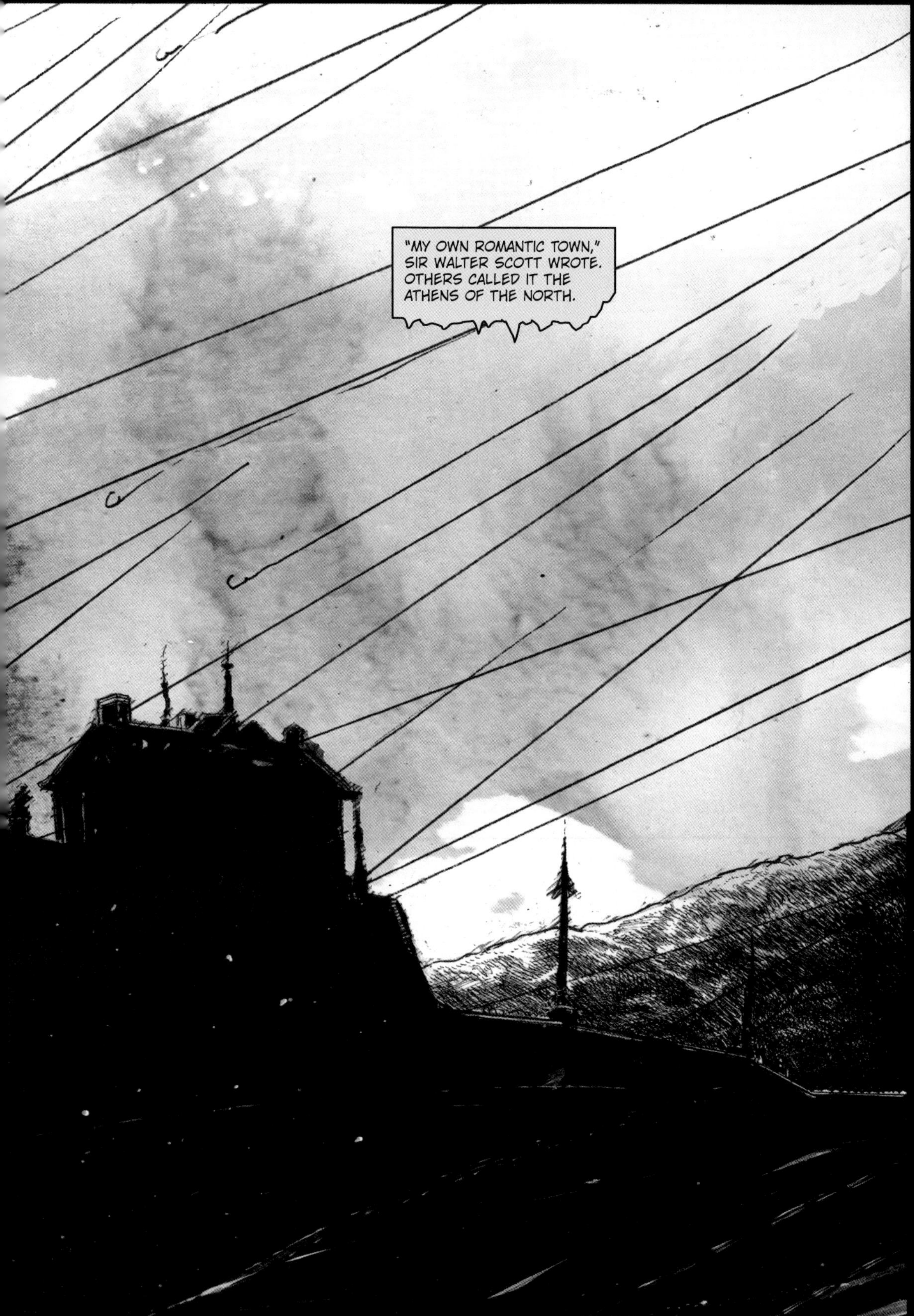
"MY OWN ROMANTIC TOWN," SIR WALTER SCOTT WROTE. OTHERS CALLED IT THE ATHENS OF THE NORTH.

CHAPTER I
THE GARGOYLE'S LAD

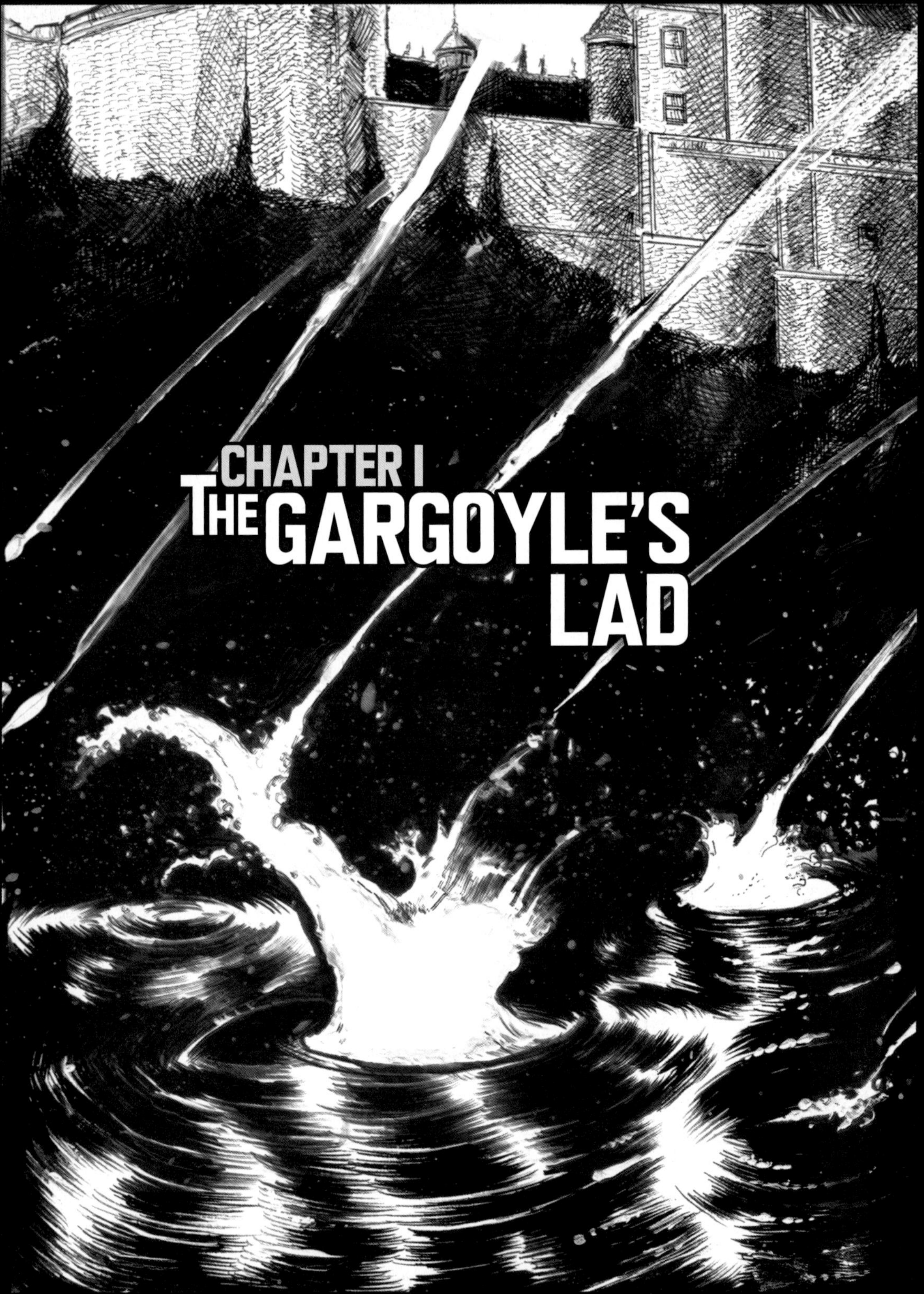

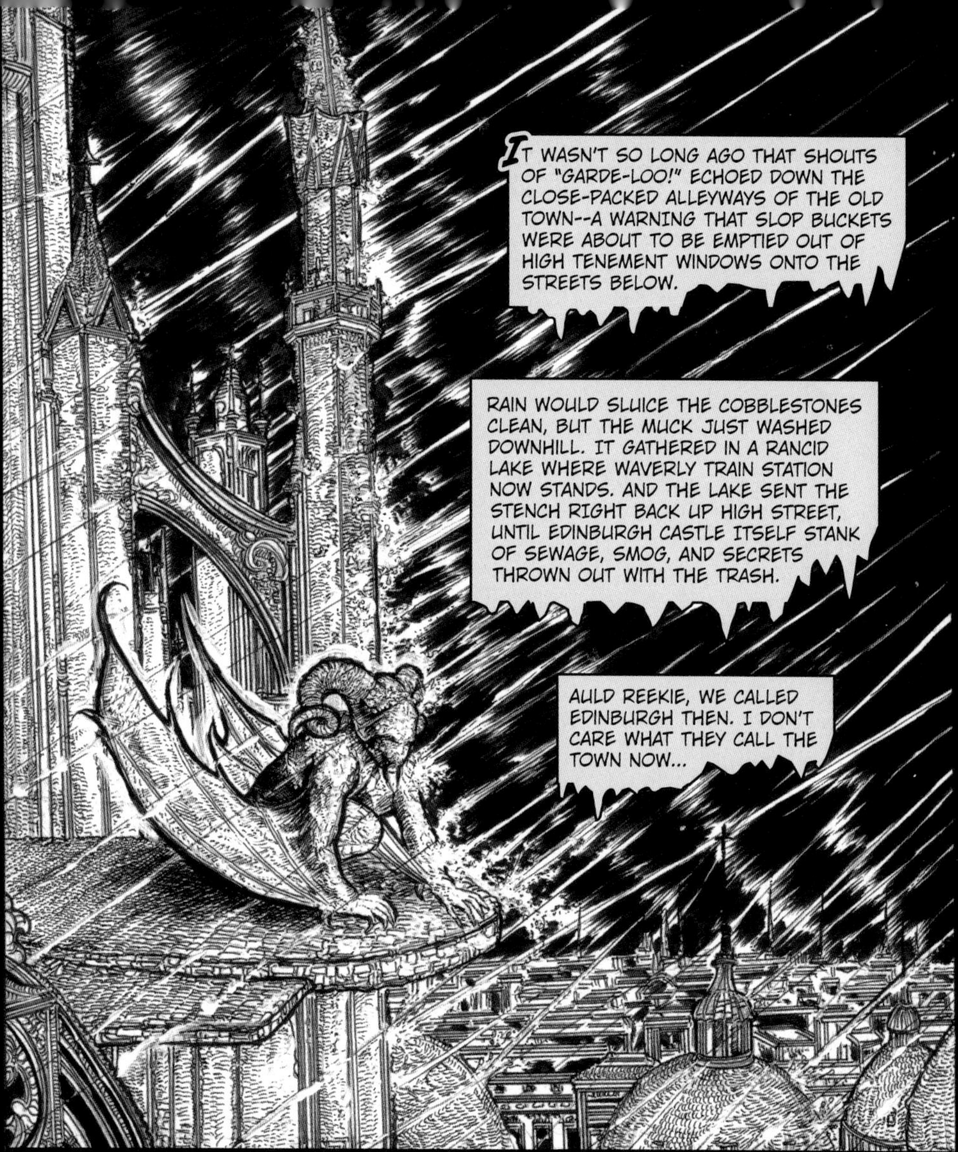
IT WASN'T SO LONG AGO THAT SHOUTS OF "GARDE-LOO!" ECHOED DOWN THE CLOSE-PACKED ALLEYWAYS OF THE OLD TOWN--A WARNING THAT SLOP BUCKETS WERE ABOUT TO BE EMPTIED OUT OF HIGH TENEMENT WINDOWS ONTO THE STREETS BELOW.
RAIN WOULD SLUICE THE COBBLESTONES CLEAN, BUT THE MUCK JUST WASHED DOWNHILL. IT GATHERED IN A RANCID LAKE WHERE WAVERLY TRAIN STATION NOW STANDS. AND THE LAKE SENT THE STENCH RIGHT BACK UP HIGH STREET, UNTIL EDINBURGH CASTLE ITSELF STANK OF SEWAGE, SMOG, AND SECRETS THROWN OUT WITH THE TRASH.
AULD REEKIE, WE CALLED EDINBURGH THEN. I DON'T CARE WHAT THEY CALL THE TOWN NOW...

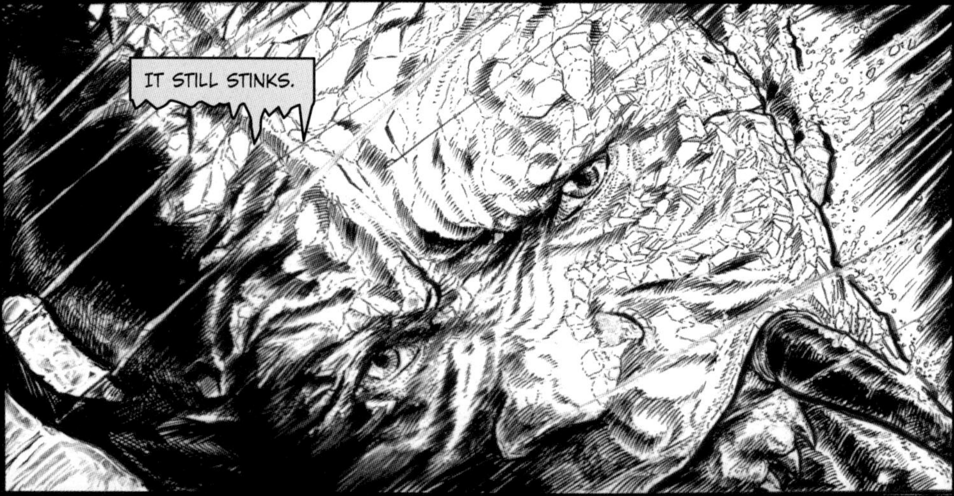
IT STILL STINKS.

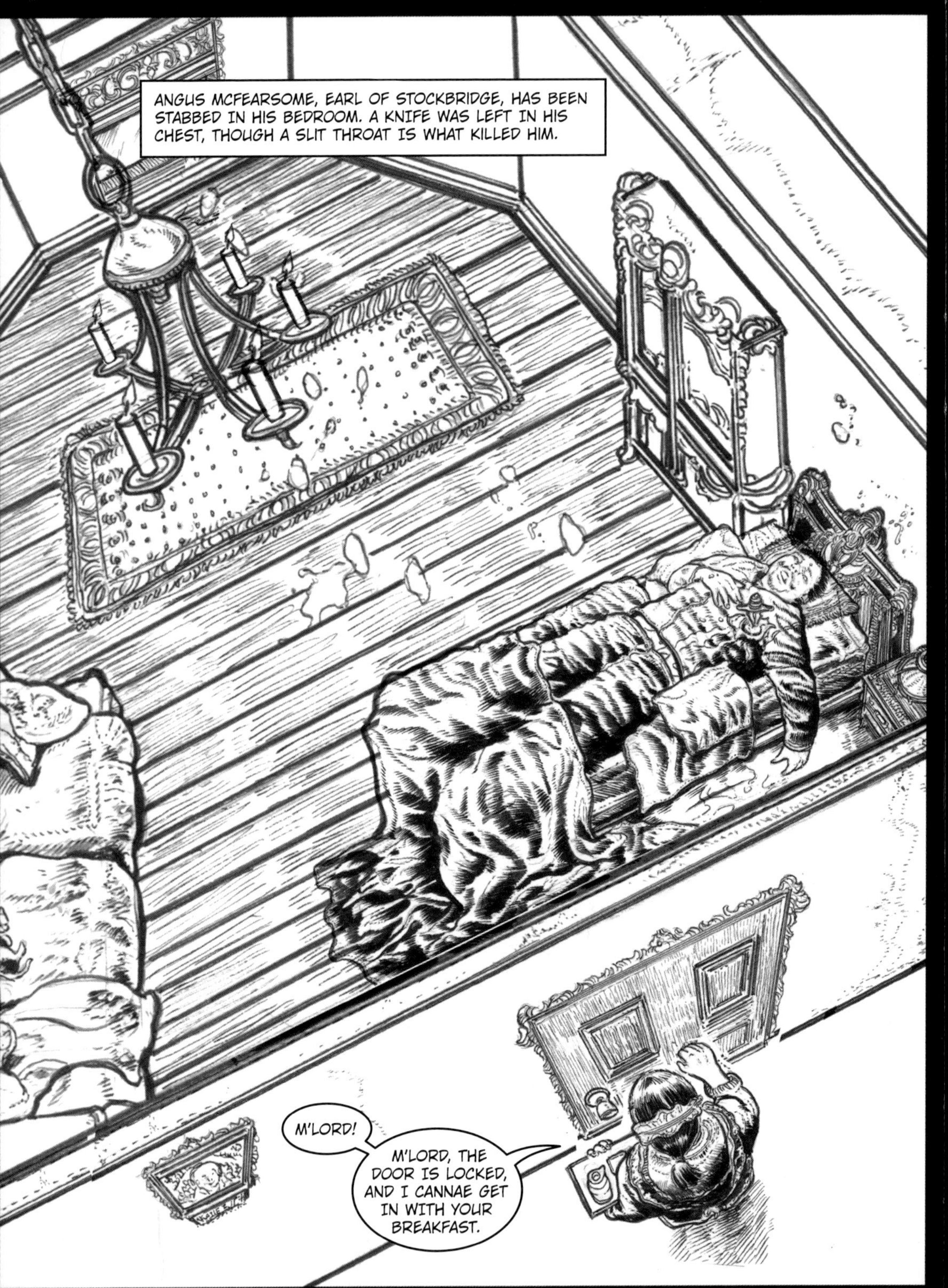
ANGUS MCFEARSOME, EARL OF STOCKBRIDGE, HAS BEEN STABBED IN HIS BEDROOM. A KNIFE WAS LEFT IN HIS CHEST, THOUGH A SLIT THROAT IS WHAT KILLED HIM.
M'LORD!
M'LORD, THE DOOR IS LOCKED, AND I CANNAE GET IN WITH YOUR BREAKFAST.

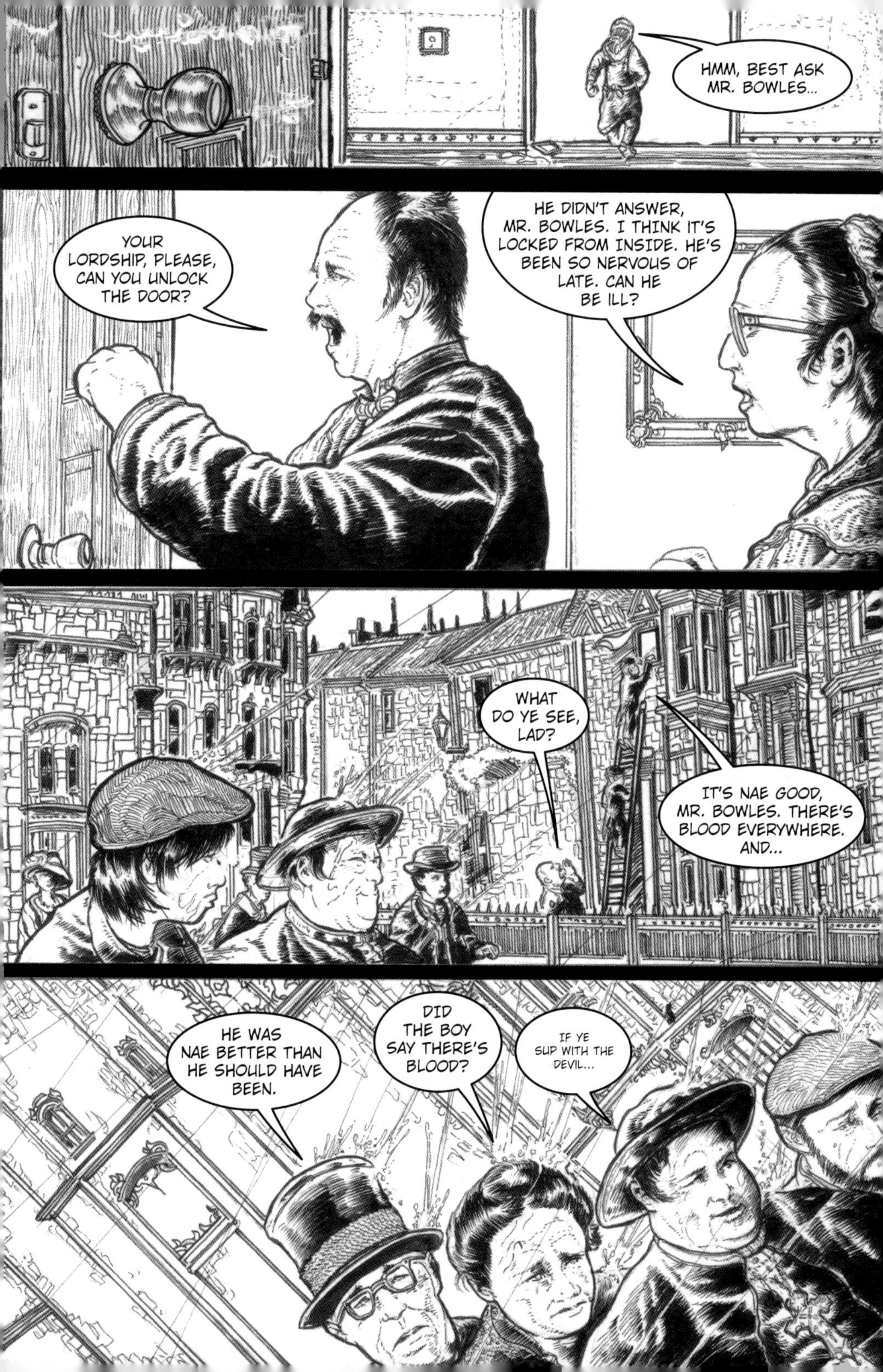
HMM, BEST ASK MR. BOWLES...
YOUR LORDSHIP, PLEASE, CAN YOU UNLOCK THE DOOR?
HE DIDN'T ANSWER, MR. BOWLES. I THINK IT'S LOCKED FROM INSIDE. HE'S BEEN SO NERVOUS OF LATE. CAN HE BE ILL?
WHAT DO YE SEE, LAD?
IT'S NAE GOOD, MR. BOWLES. THERE'S BLOOD EVERYWHERE. AND...
HE WAS NAE BETTER THAN HE SHOULD HAVE BEEN.
DID THE BOY SAY THERE'S BLOOD?
IF YE SUP WITH THE DEVIL...

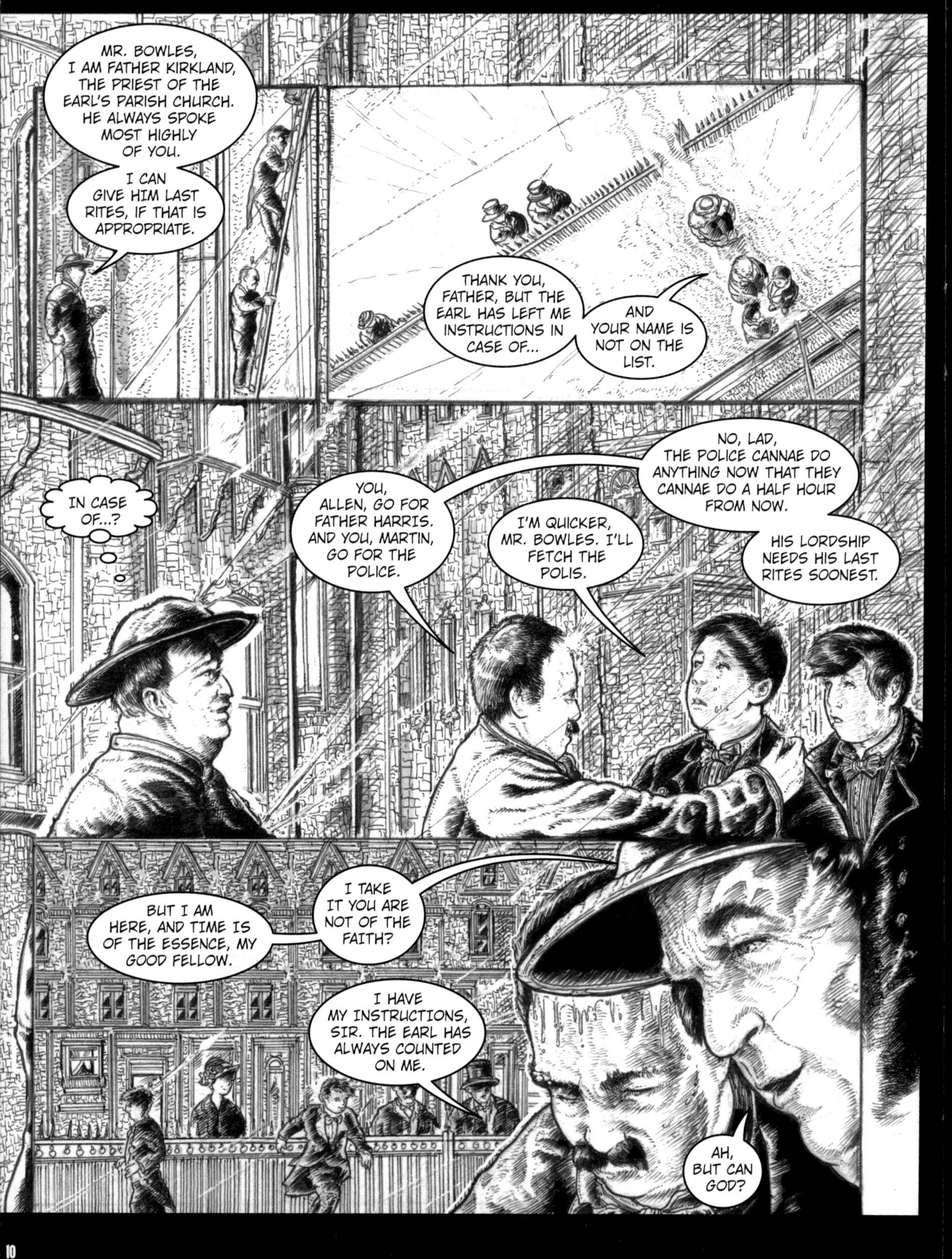
MR. BOWLES, I AM FATHER KIRKLAND, THE PRIEST OF THE EARL'S PARISH CHURCH. HE ALWAYS SPOKE MOST HIGHLY OF YOU.
I CAN GIVE HIM LAST RITES, IF THAT IS APPROPRIATE.
THANK YOU, FATHER, BUT THE EARL HAS LEFT ME INSTRUCTIONS IN CASE OF...
AND YOUR NAME IS NOT ON THE LIST.
IN CASE OF...?
YOU, ALLEN, GO FOR FATHER HARRIS. AND YOU, MARTIN, GO FOR THE POLICE.
I'M QUICKER, MR. BOWLES. I'LL FETCH THE POLIS.
NO, LAD, THE POLICE CANNAE DO ANYTHING NOW THAT THEY CANNAE DO A HALF HOUR FROM NOW.
HIS LORDSHIP NEEDS HIS LAST RITES SOONEST.
BUT I AM HERE, AND TIME IS OF THE ESSENCE, MY GOOD FELLOW.
I TAKE IT YOU ARE NOT OF THE FAITH?
I HAVE MY INSTRUCTIONS, SIR. THE EARL HAS ALWAYS COUNTED ON ME.
AH, BUT CAN GOD?

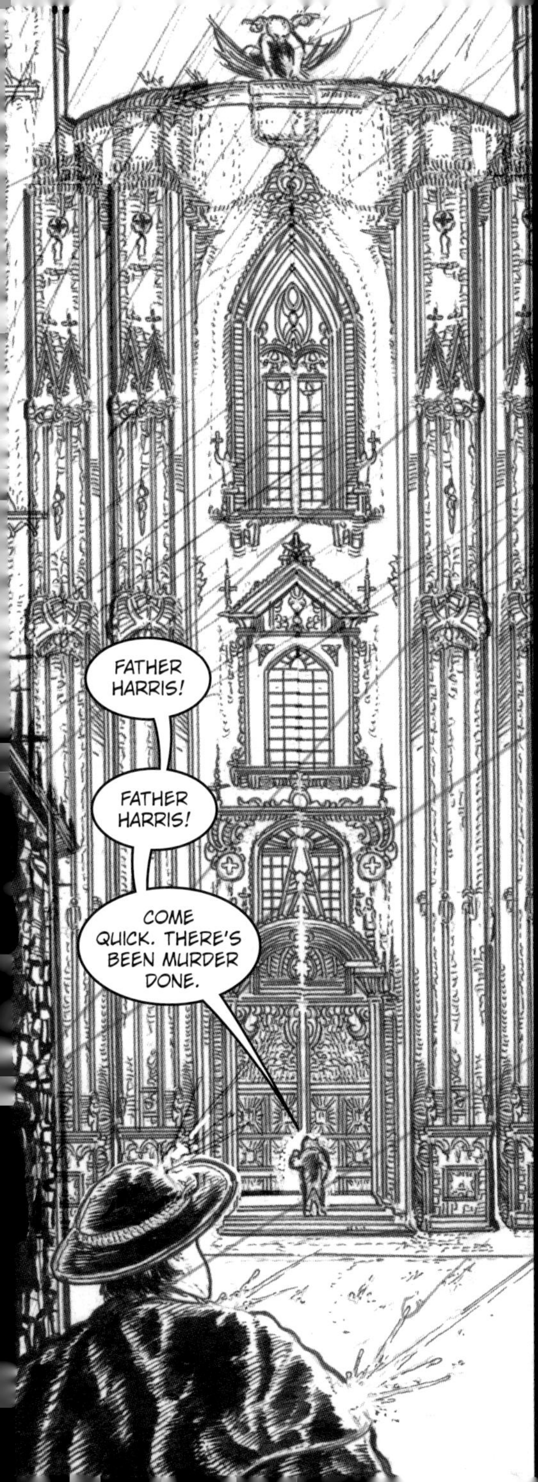
FATHER HARRIS!
FATHER HARRIS!
COME QUICK. THERE'S BEEN MURDER DONE.
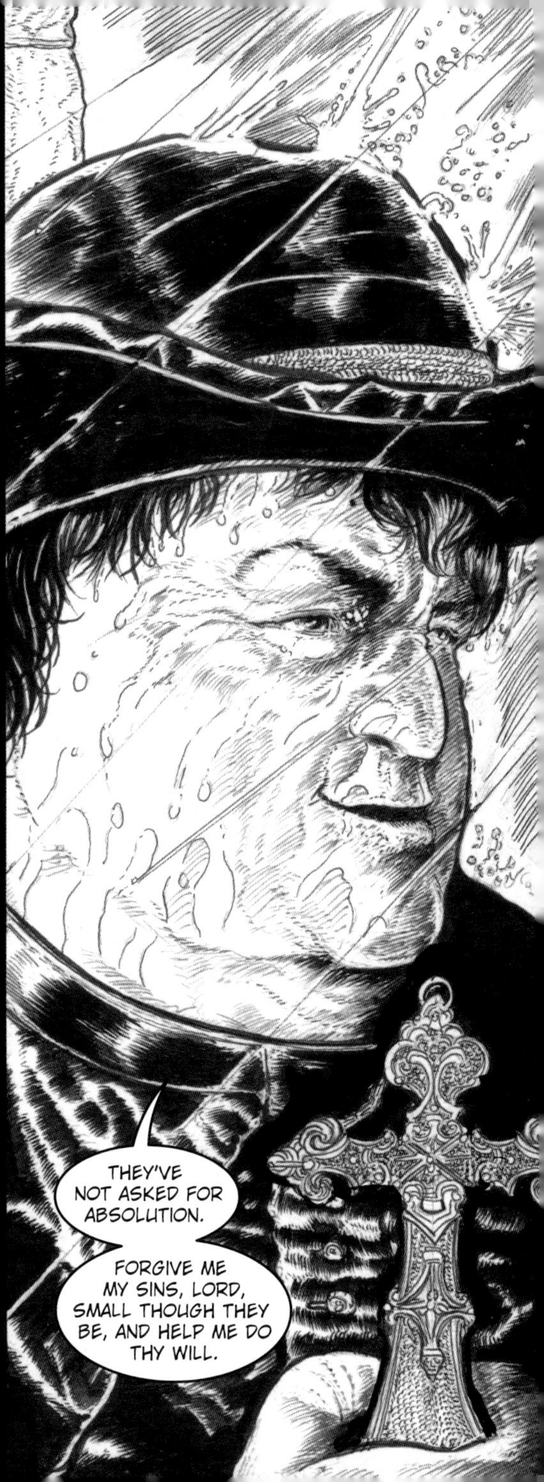
THEY'VE NOT ASKED FOR ABSOLUTION.
FORGIVE ME MY SINS, LORD, SMALL THOUGH THEY BE, AND HELP ME DO THY WILL.

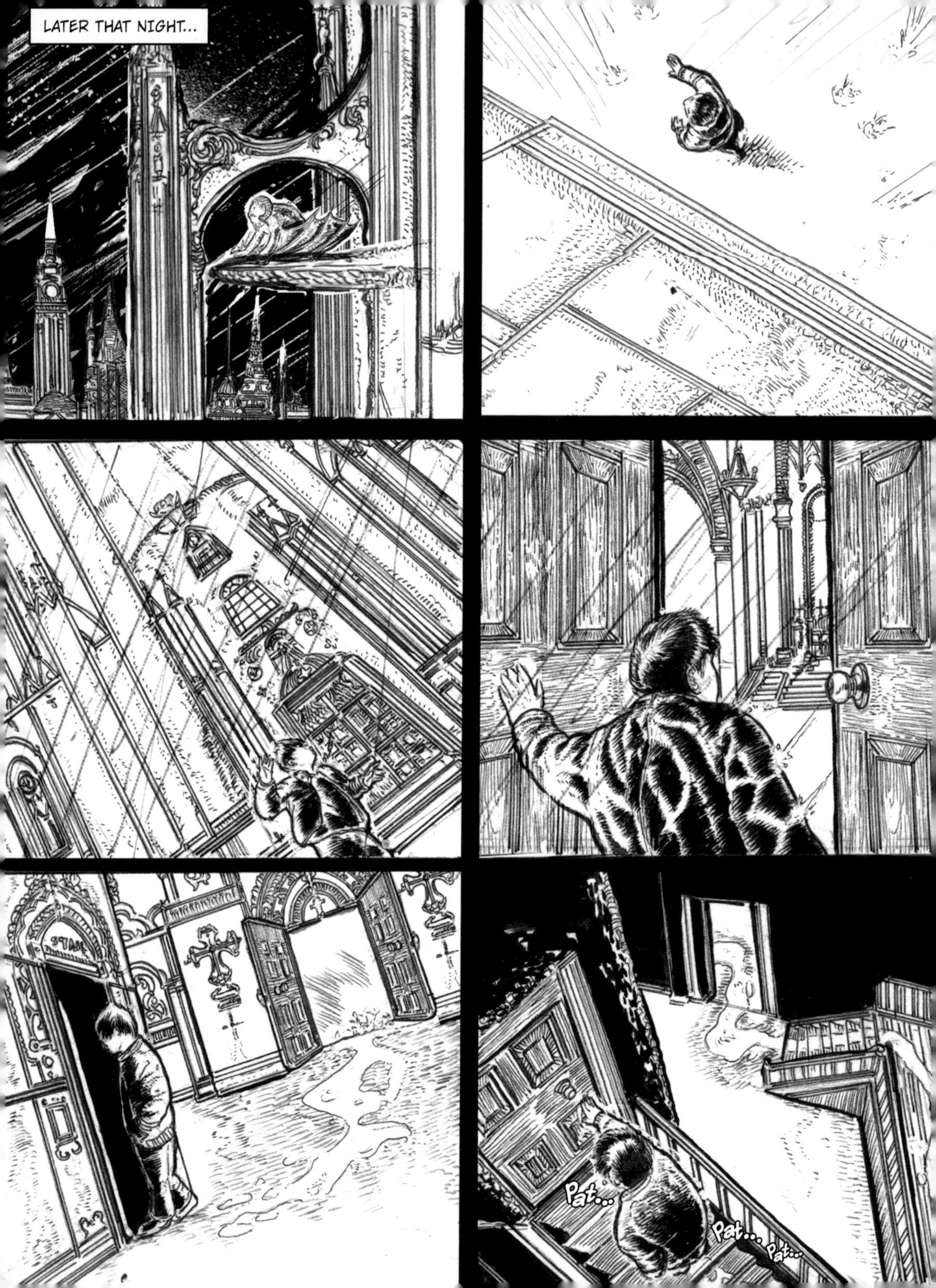
LATER THAT NIGHT...
Pat...
Pat... Pat...

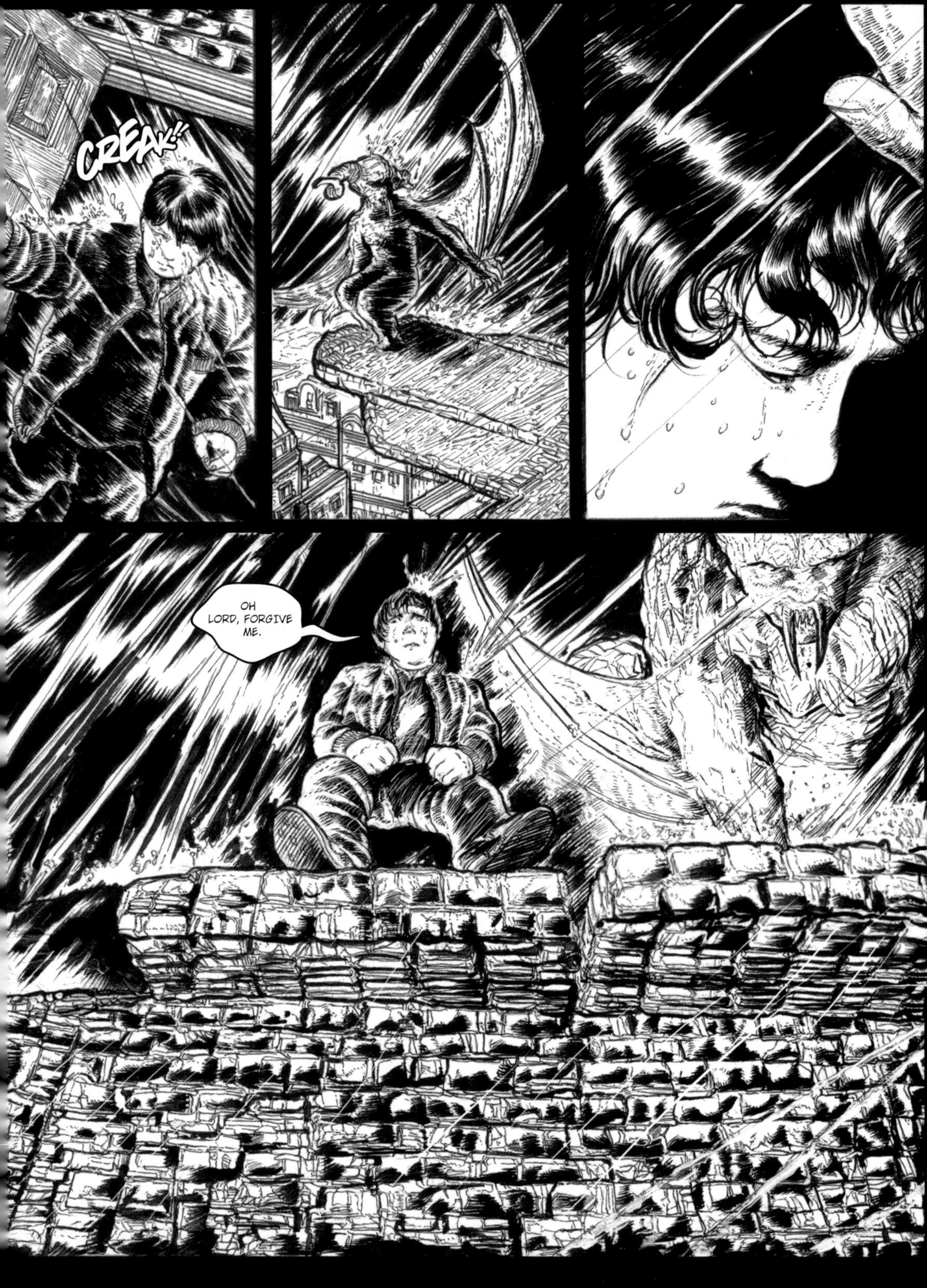
CREAK!!
OH LORD, FORGIVE ME.

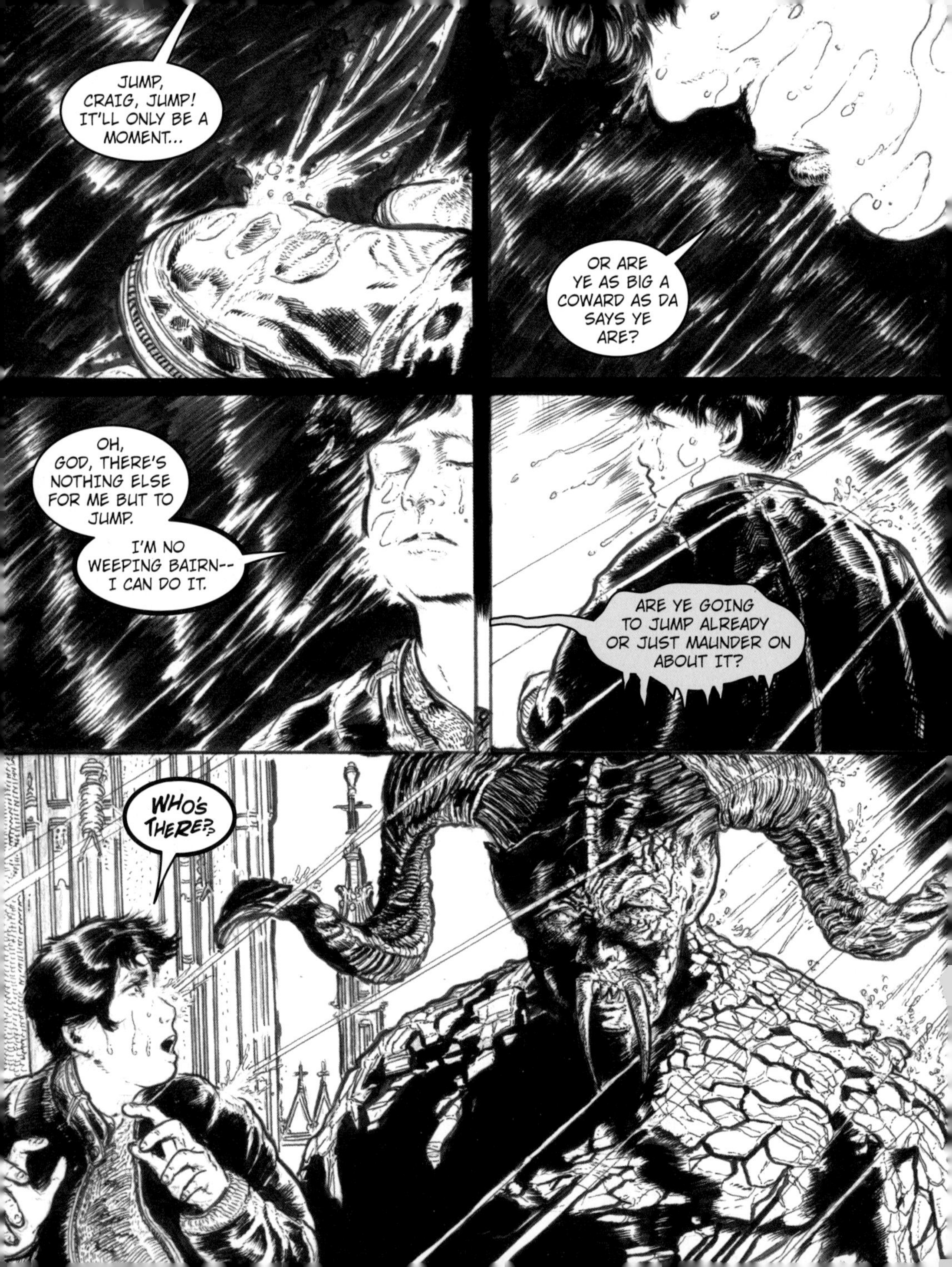
JUMP, CRAIG, JUMP! IT'LL ONLY BE A MOMENT...
OR ARE YE AS BIG A COWARD AS DA SAYS YE ARE?
OH, GOD, THERE'S NOTHING ELSE FOR ME BUT TO JUMP.
I'M NO WEEPING BAIRN-- I CAN DO IT.
ARE YE GOING TO JUMP ALREADY OR JUST MAUNDER ON ABOUT IT?
WHO'S THERE?

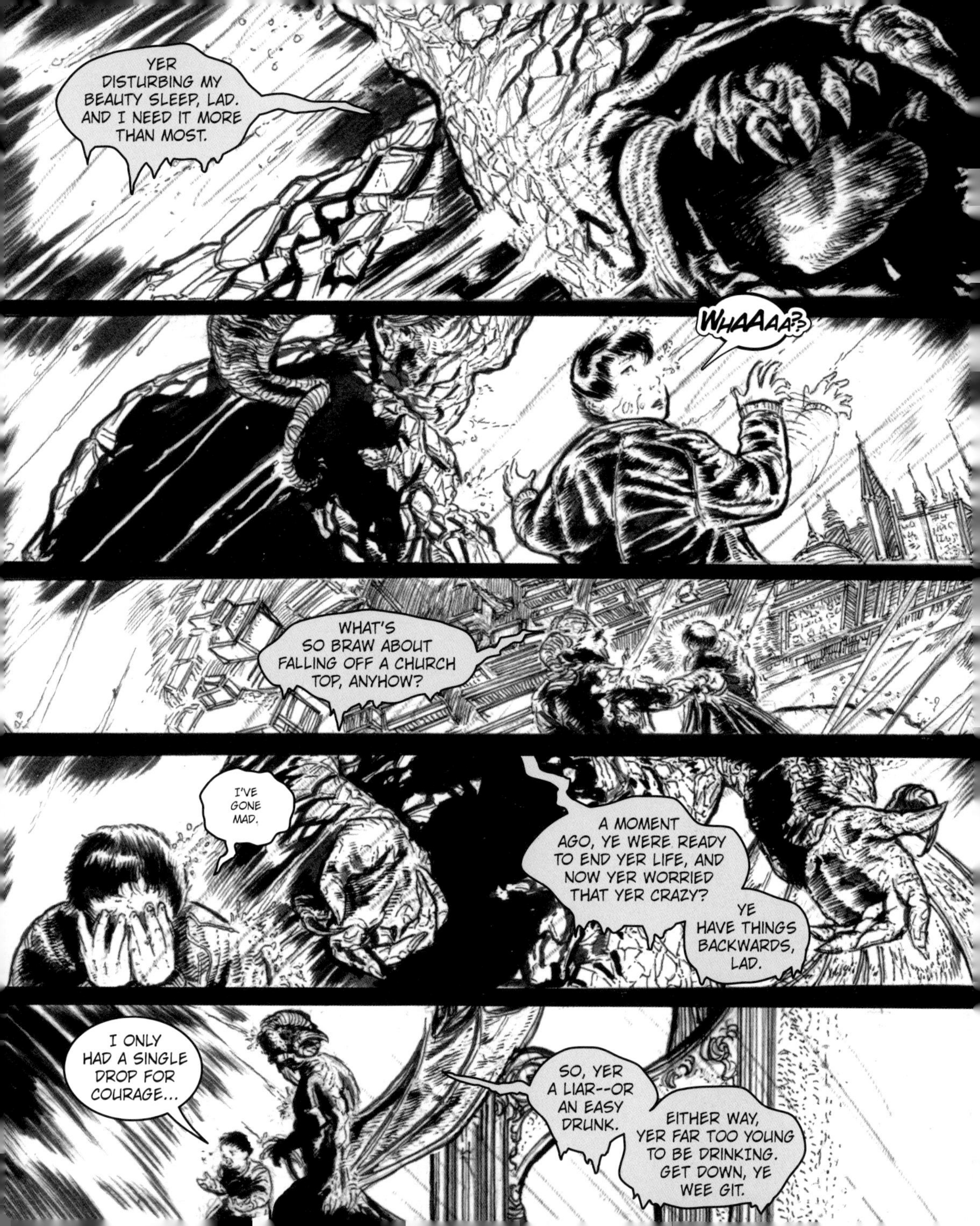
YER DISTURBING MY BEAUTY SLEEP, LAD. AND I NEED IT MORE THAN MOST.
WHAAAA?
WHAT'S SO BRAW ABOUT FALLING OFF A CHURCH TOP, ANYHOW?
I'VE GONE MAD.
A MOMENT AGO, YE WERE READY TO END YER LIFE, AND NOW YER WORRIED THAT YER CRAZY?
YE HAVE THINGS BACKWARDS, LAD.
I ONLY HAD A SINGLE DROP FOR COURAGE...
SO, YER A LIAR--OR AN EASY DRUNK.
EITHER WAY, YER FAR TOO YOUNG TO BE DRINKING. GET DOWN, YE WEE GIT.

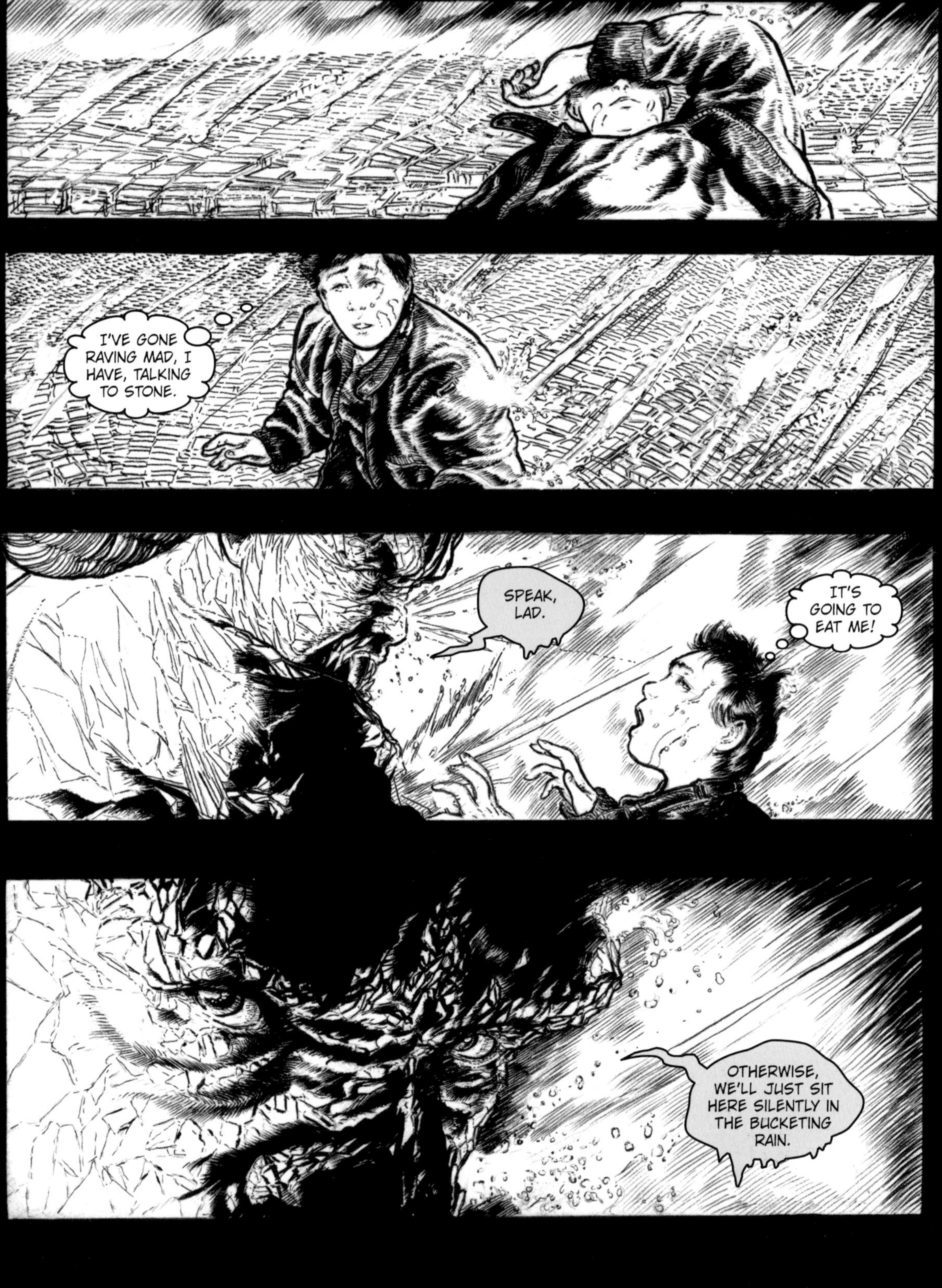

I'VE GONE RAVING MAD, I HAVE, TALKING TO STONE.
SPEAK, LAD.
IT'S GOING TO EAT ME!
OTHERWISE, WE'LL JUST SIT HERE SILENTLY IN THE BUCKETING RAIN.

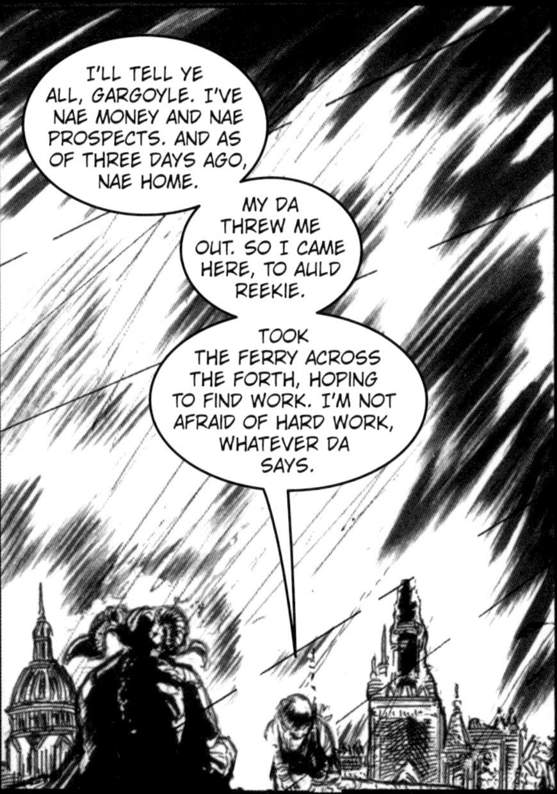
I'LL TELL YE ALL, GARGOYLE. I'VE NAE MONEY AND NAE PROSPECTS. AND AS OF THREE DAYS AGO, NAE HOME.
MY DA THREW ME OUT. SO I CAME HERE, TO AULD REEKIE.
TOOK THE FERRY ACROSS THE FORTH, HOPING TO FIND WORK. I'M NOT AFRAID OF HARD WORK, WHATEVER DA SAYS.

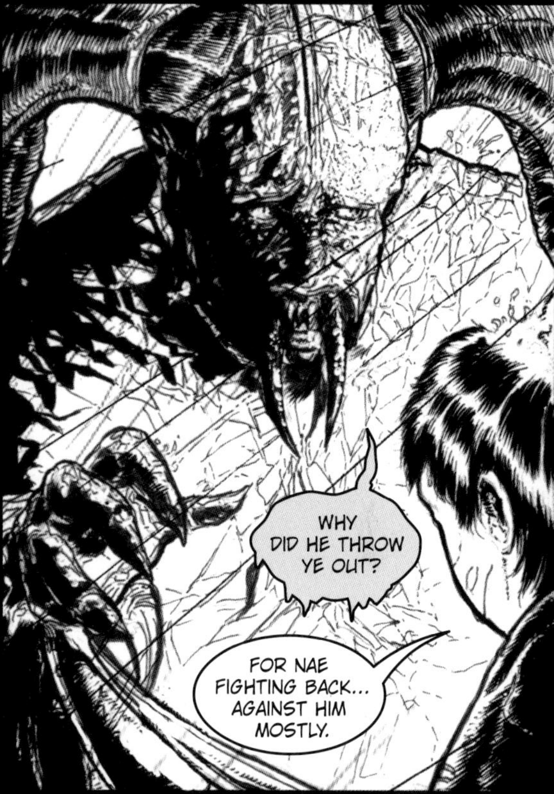
WHY DID HE THROW YE OUT?
FOR NAE FIGHTING BACK... AGAINST HIM MOSTLY.

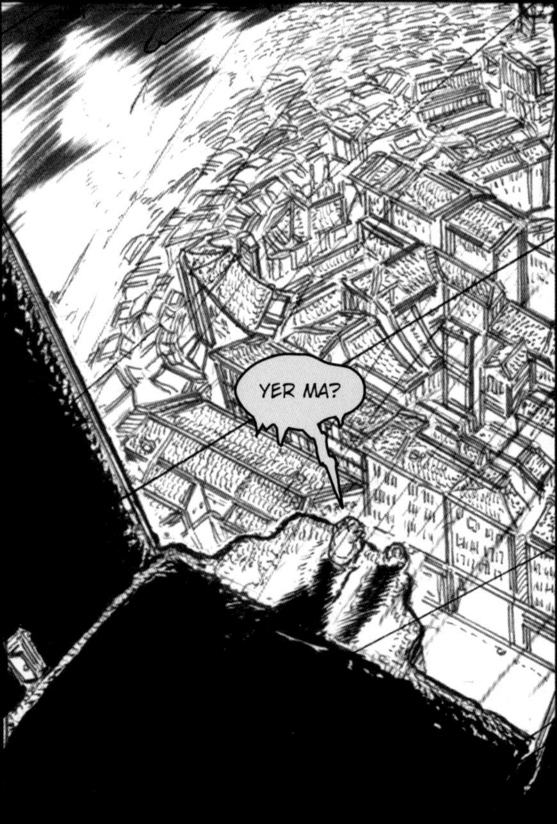
YER MA?

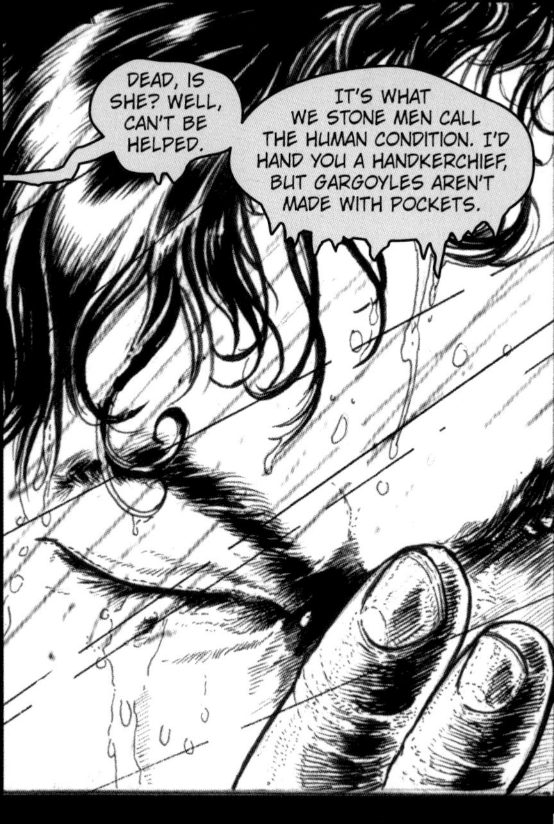
DEAD, IS SHE? WELL, CAN'T BE HELPED.
IT'S WHAT WE STONE MEN CALL THE HUMAN CONDITION. I'D HAND YOU A HANDKERCHIEF, BUT GARGOYLES AREN'T MADE WITH POCKETS.

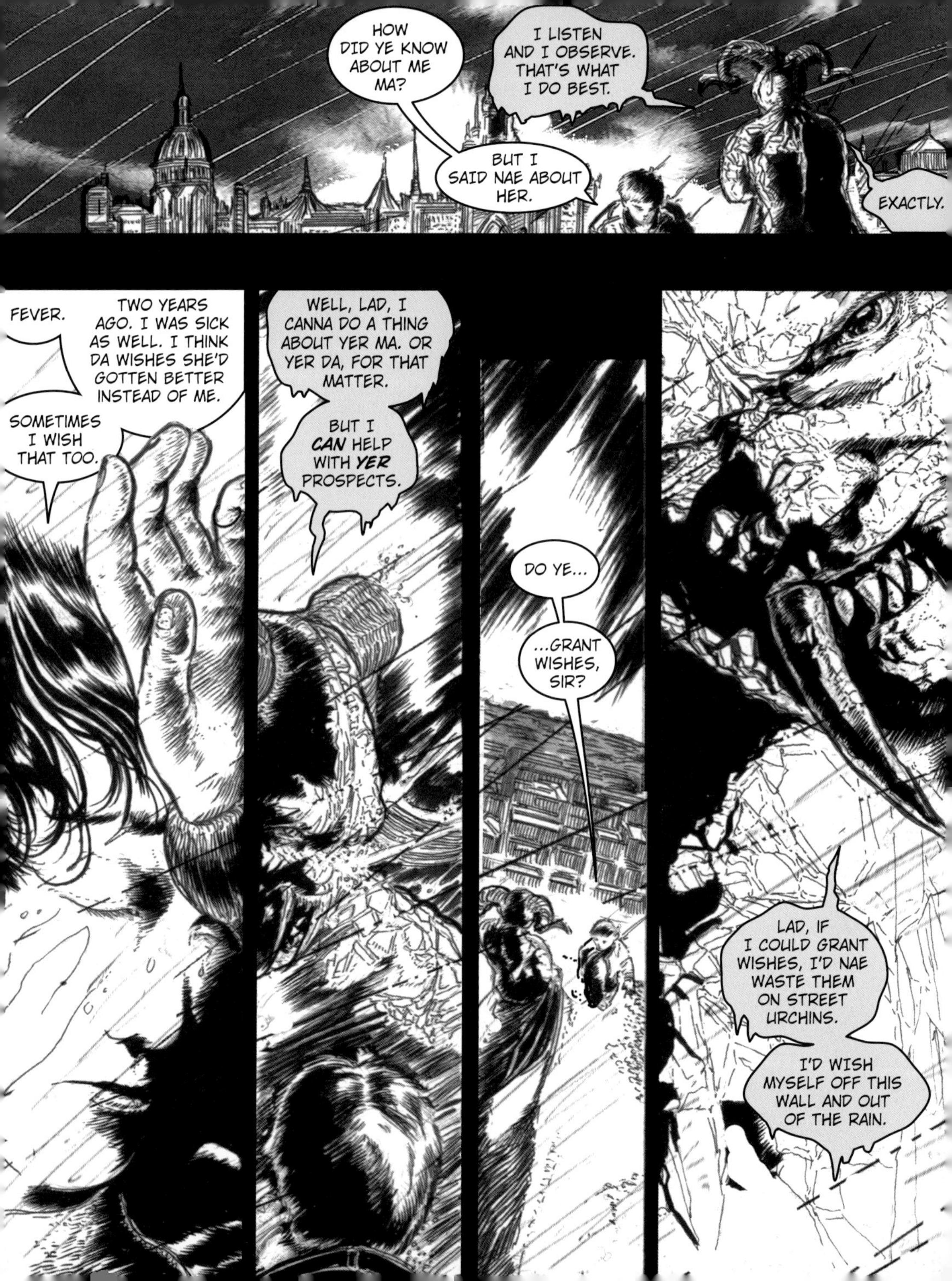
HOW DID YE KNOW ABOUT ME MA?
I LISTEN AND I OBSERVE. THAT'S WHAT I DO BEST.
BUT I SAID NAE ABOUT HER.
EXACTLY.
FEVER.
TWO YEARS AGO. I WAS SICK AS WELL. I THINK DA WISHES SHE'D GOTTEN BETTER INSTEAD OF ME.
SOMETIMES I WISH THAT TOO.
WELL, LAD, I CANNA DO A THING ABOUT YER MA. OR YER DA, FOR THAT MATTER.
BUT I CAN HELP WITH YER PROSPECTS.
DO YE...
...GRANT WISHES, SIR?
LAD, IF I COULD GRANT WISHES, I'D NAE WASTE THEM ON STREET URCHINS.
I'D WISH MYSELF OFF THIS WALL AND OUT OF THE RAIN.

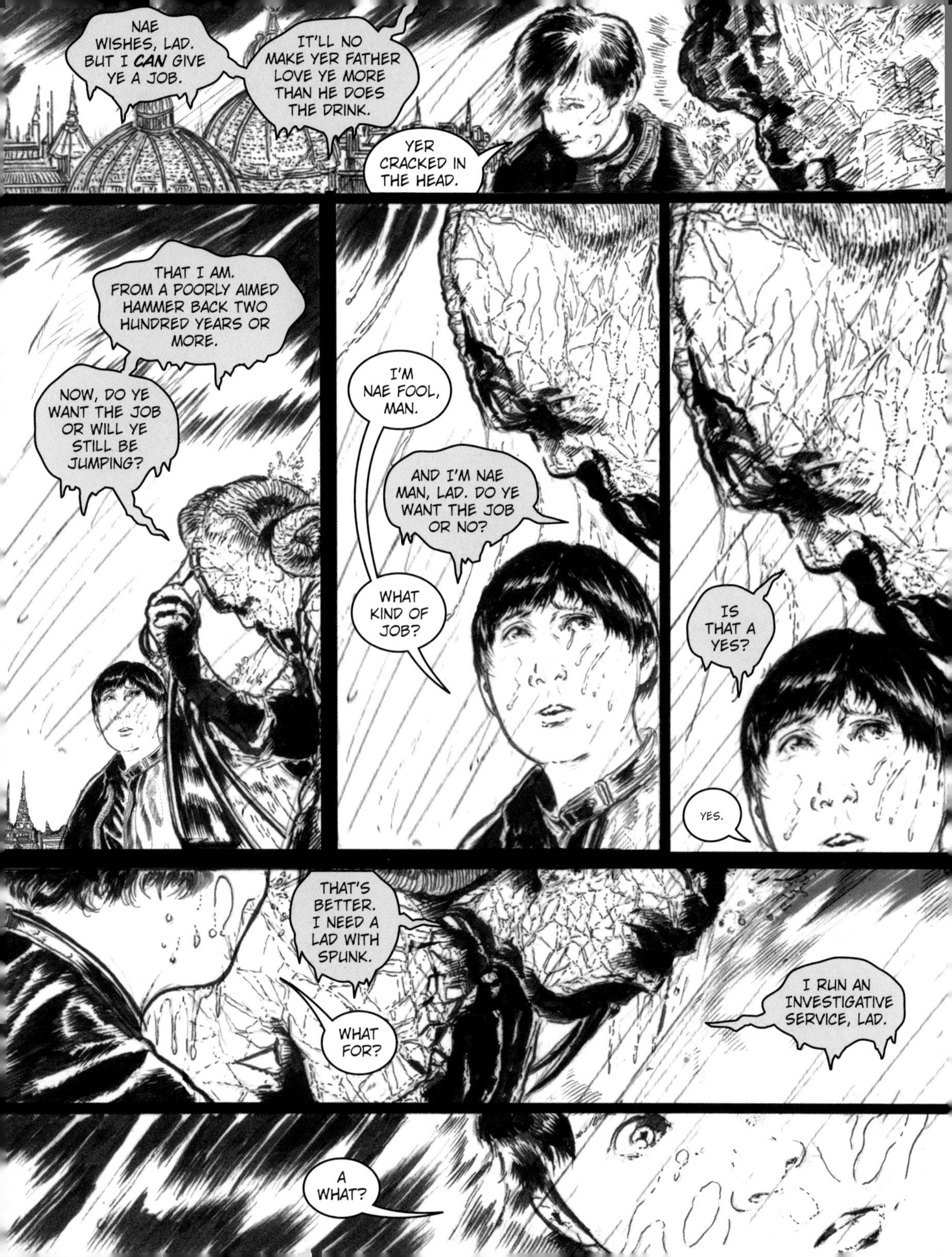
NAE WISHES, LAD. BUT I CAN GIVE YE A JOB.
IT'LL NO MAKE YER FATHER LOVE YE MORE THAN HE DOES THE DRINK.
YER CRACKED IN THE HEAD.
THAT I AM. FROM A POORLY AIMED HAMMER BACK TWO HUNDRED YEARS OR MORE.
NOW, DO YE WANT THE JOB OR WILL YE STILL BE JUMPING?
I'M NAE FOOL, MAN.
AND I'M NAE MAN, LAD. DO YE WANT THE JOB OR NO?
WHAT KIND OF JOB?
IS THAT A YES?
YES.
THAT'S BETTER. I NEED A LAD WITH SPUNK.
WHAT FOR?
I RUN AN INVESTIGATIVE SERVICE, LAD.
A WHAT?

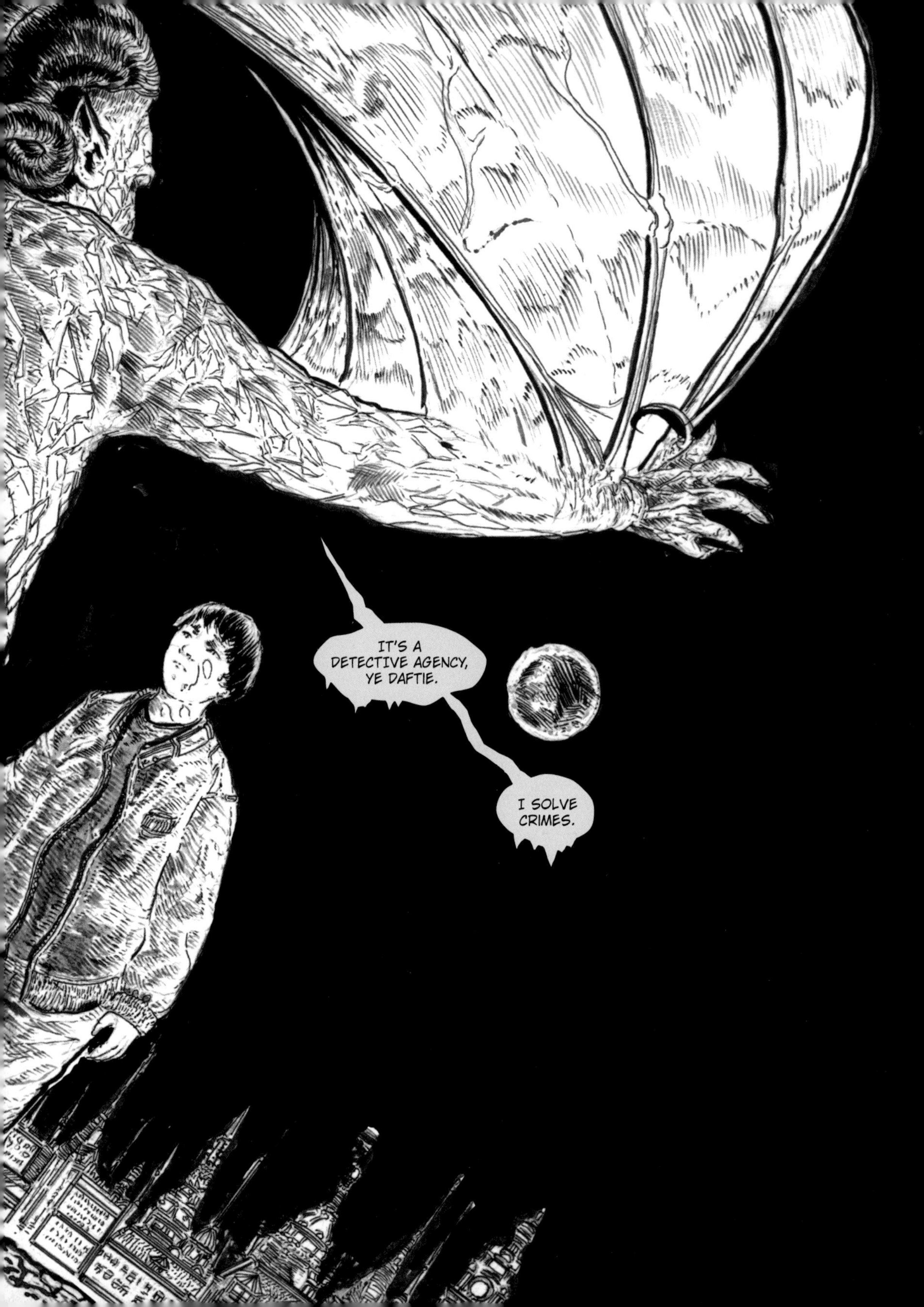
IT'S A DETECTIVE AGENCY, YE DAFTIE.
I SOLVE CRIMES.

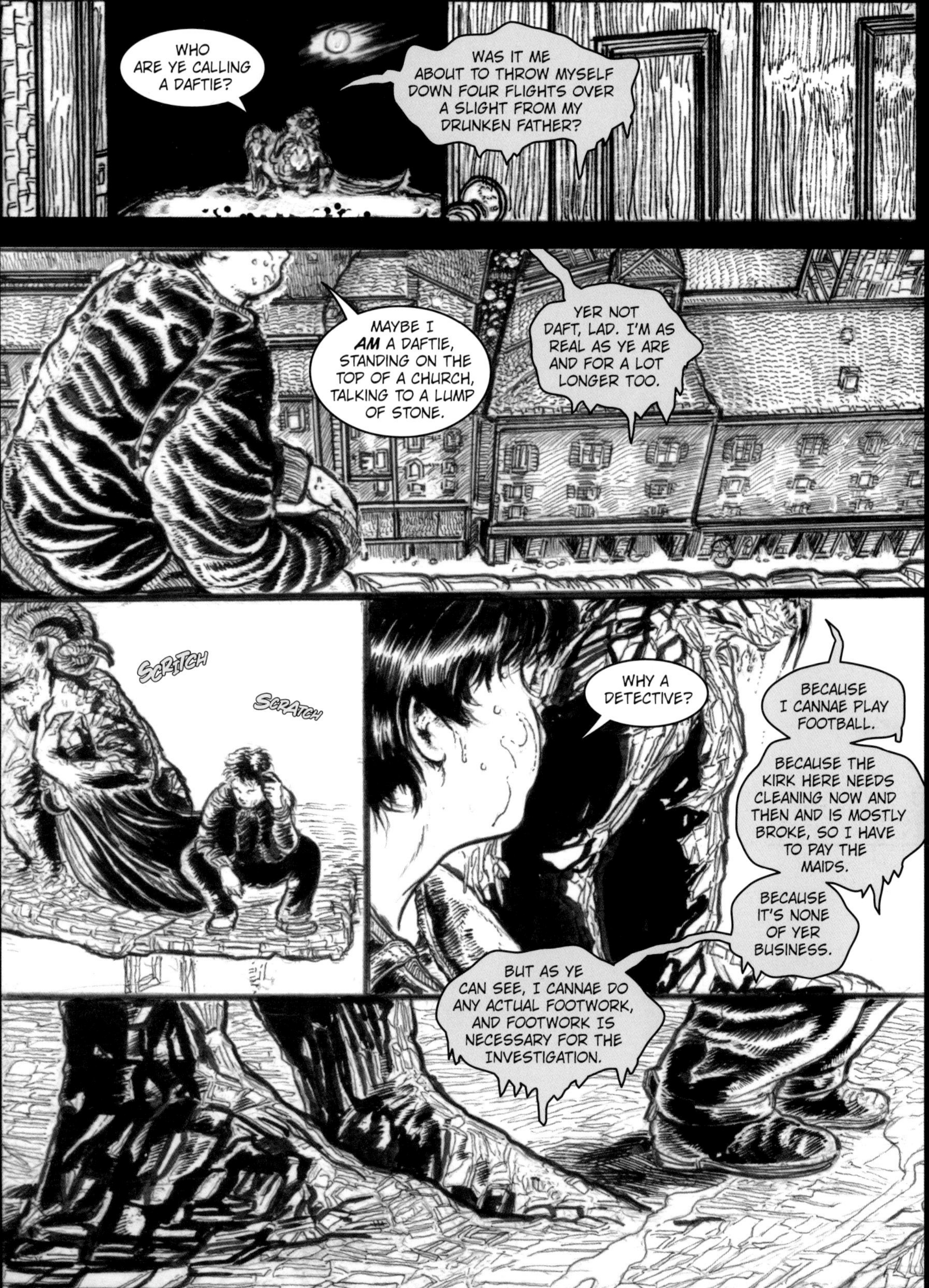
WHO ARE YE CALLING A DAFTIE?
WAS IT ME ABOUT TO THROW MYSELF DOWN FOUR FLIGHTS OVER A SLIGHT FROM MY DRUNKEN FATHER?
MAYBE I **AM** A DAFTIE, STANDING ON THE TOP OF A CHURCH, TALKING TO A LUMP OF STONE.
YER NOT DAFT, LAD. I'M AS REAL AS YE ARE AND FOR A LOT LONGER TOO.
SCRITCH
SCRATCH
WHY A DETECTIVE?
BECAUSE I CANNAE PLAY FOOTBALL.
BECAUSE THE KIRK HERE NEEDS CLEANING NOW AND THEN AND IS MOSTLY BROKE, SO I HAVE TO PAY THE MAIDS.
BECAUSE IT'S NONE OF YER BUSINESS.
BUT AS YE CAN SEE, I CANNAE DO ANY ACTUAL FOOTWORK, AND FOOTWORK IS NECESSARY FOR THE INVESTIGATION.

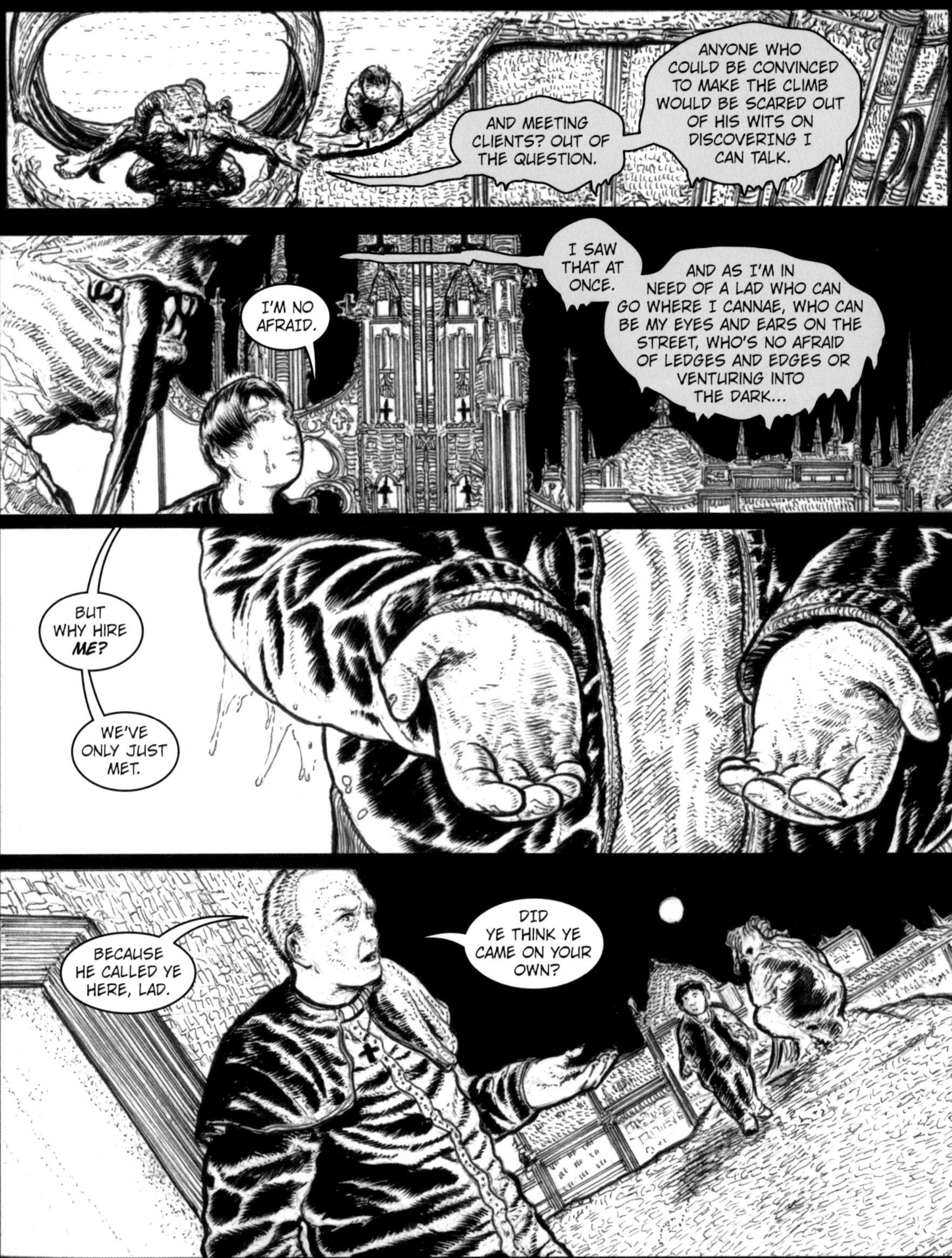

ANYONE WHO COULD BE CONVINCED TO MAKE THE CLIMB WOULD BE SCARED OUT OF HIS WITS ON DISCOVERING I CAN TALK.
AND MEETING CLIENTS? OUT OF THE QUESTION.
I'M NO AFRAID.
I SAW THAT AT ONCE.
AND AS I'M IN NEED OF A LAD WHO CAN GO WHERE I CANNAE, WHO CAN BE MY EYES AND EARS ON THE STREET, WHO'S NO AFRAID OF LEDGES AND EDGES OR VENTURING INTO THE DARK...
BUT WHY HIRE ***ME?***
WE'VE ONLY JUST MET.
BECAUSE HE CALLED YE HERE, LAD.
DID YE THINK YE CAME ON YOUR OWN?

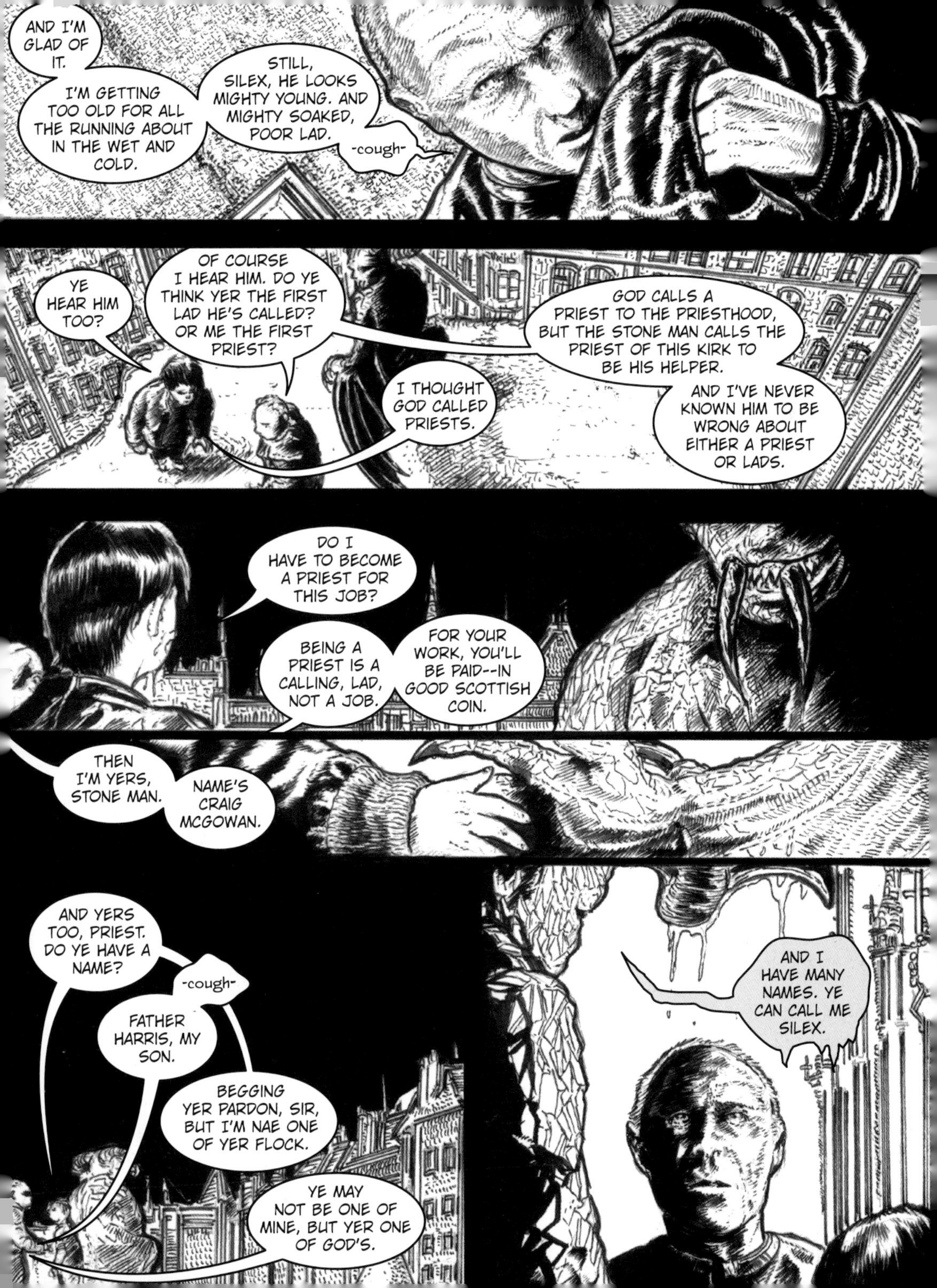
AND I'M GLAD OF IT.
I'M GETTING TOO OLD FOR ALL THE RUNNING ABOUT IN THE WET AND COLD.
STILL, SILEX, HE LOOKS MIGHTY YOUNG. AND MIGHTY SOAKED, POOR LAD.
-cough-
YE HEAR HIM TOO?
OF COURSE I HEAR HIM. DO YE THINK YER THE FIRST LAD HE'S CALLED? OR ME THE FIRST PRIEST?
I THOUGHT GOD CALLED PRIESTS.
GOD CALLS A PRIEST TO THE PRIESTHOOD, BUT THE STONE MAN CALLS THE PRIEST OF THIS KIRK TO BE HIS HELPER.
AND I'VE NEVER KNOWN HIM TO BE WRONG ABOUT EITHER A PRIEST OR LADS.
DO I HAVE TO BECOME A PRIEST FOR THIS JOB?
BEING A PRIEST IS A CALLING, LAD, NOT A JOB.
FOR YOUR WORK, YOU'LL BE PAID--IN GOOD SCOTTISH COIN.
THEN I'M YERS, STONE MAN.
NAME'S CRAIG MCGOWAN.
AND YERS TOO, PRIEST. DO YE HAVE A NAME?
-cough-
FATHER HARRIS, MY SON.
BEGGING YER PARDON, SIR, BUT I'M NAE ONE OF YER FLOCK.
YE MAY NOT BE ONE OF MINE, BUT YER ONE OF GOD'S.
AND I HAVE MANY NAMES. YE CAN CALL ME SILEX.

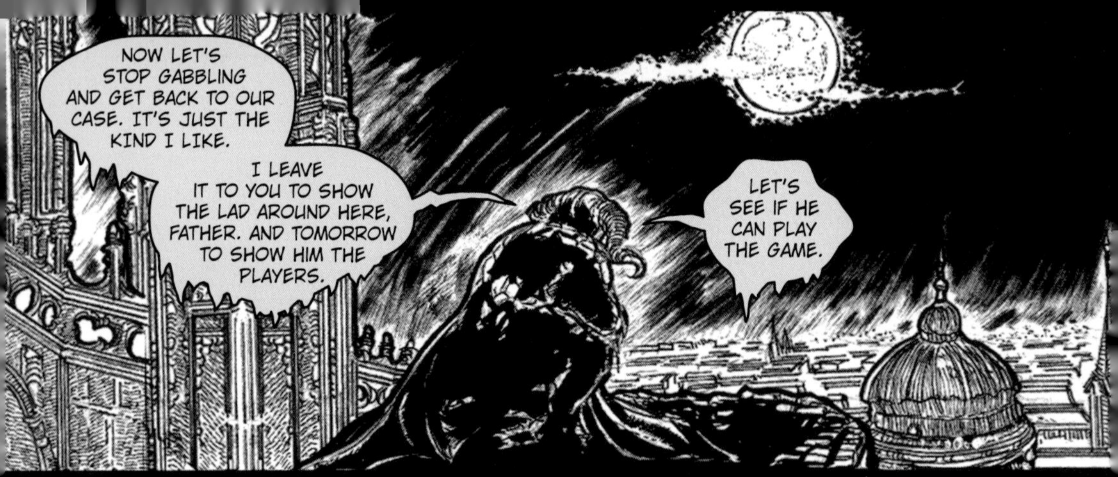
NOW LET'S STOP GABBLING AND GET BACK TO OUR CASE. IT'S JUST THE KIND I LIKE.
I LEAVE IT TO YOU TO SHOW THE LAD AROUND HERE, FATHER. AND TOMORROW TO SHOW HIM THE PLAYERS.
LET'S SEE IF HE CAN PLAY THE GAME.

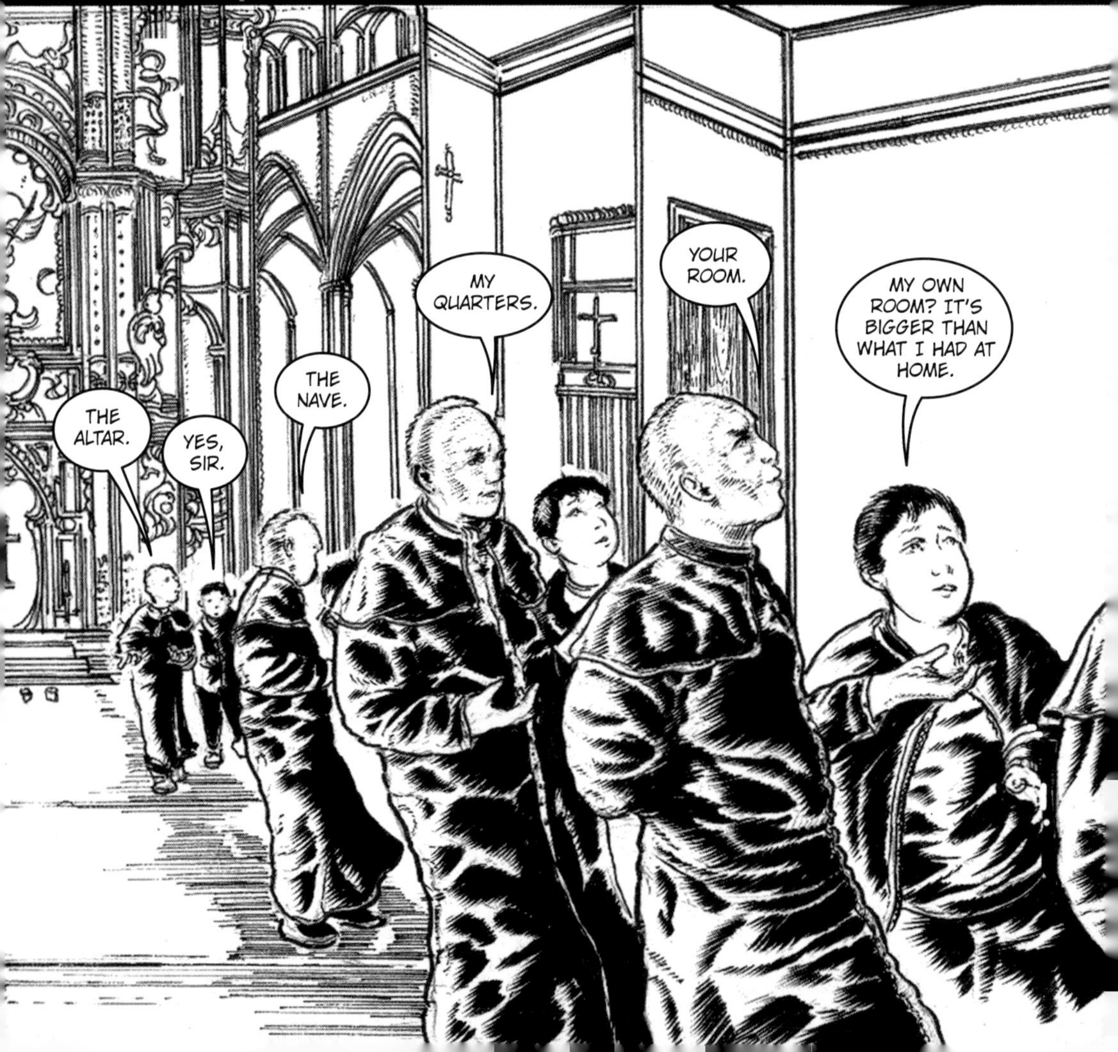
THE ALTAR.
YES, SIR.
THE NAVE.
MY QUARTERS.
YOUR ROOM.
MY OWN ROOM? IT'S BIGGER THAN WHAT I HAD AT HOME.

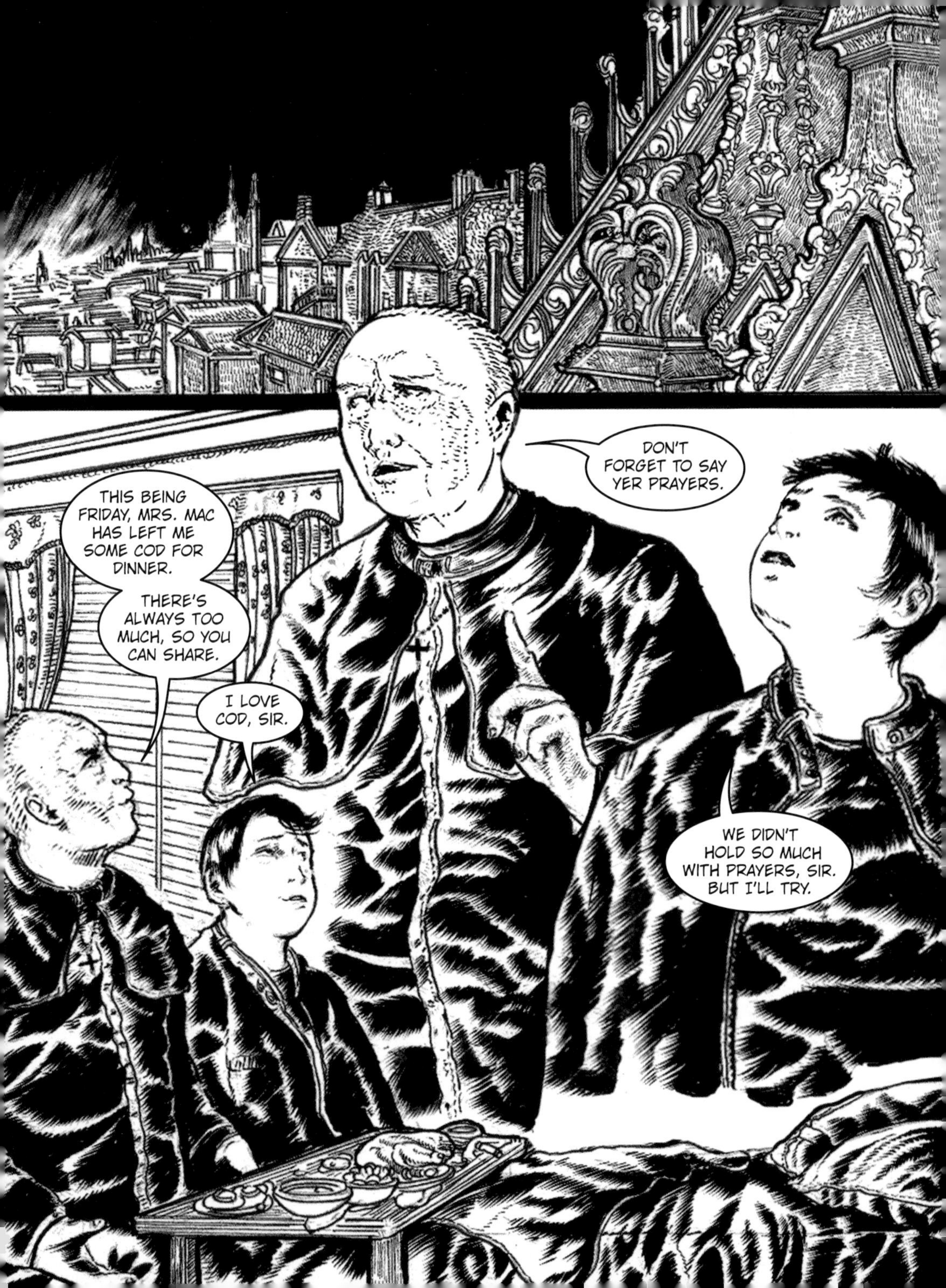
THIS BEING FRIDAY, MRS. MAC HAS LEFT ME SOME COD FOR DINNER.
THERE'S ALWAYS TOO MUCH, SO YOU CAN SHARE.
I LOVE COD, SIR.
DON'T FORGET TO SAY YER PRAYERS.
WE DIDN'T HOLD SO MUCH WITH PRAYERS, SIR. BUT I'LL TRY.

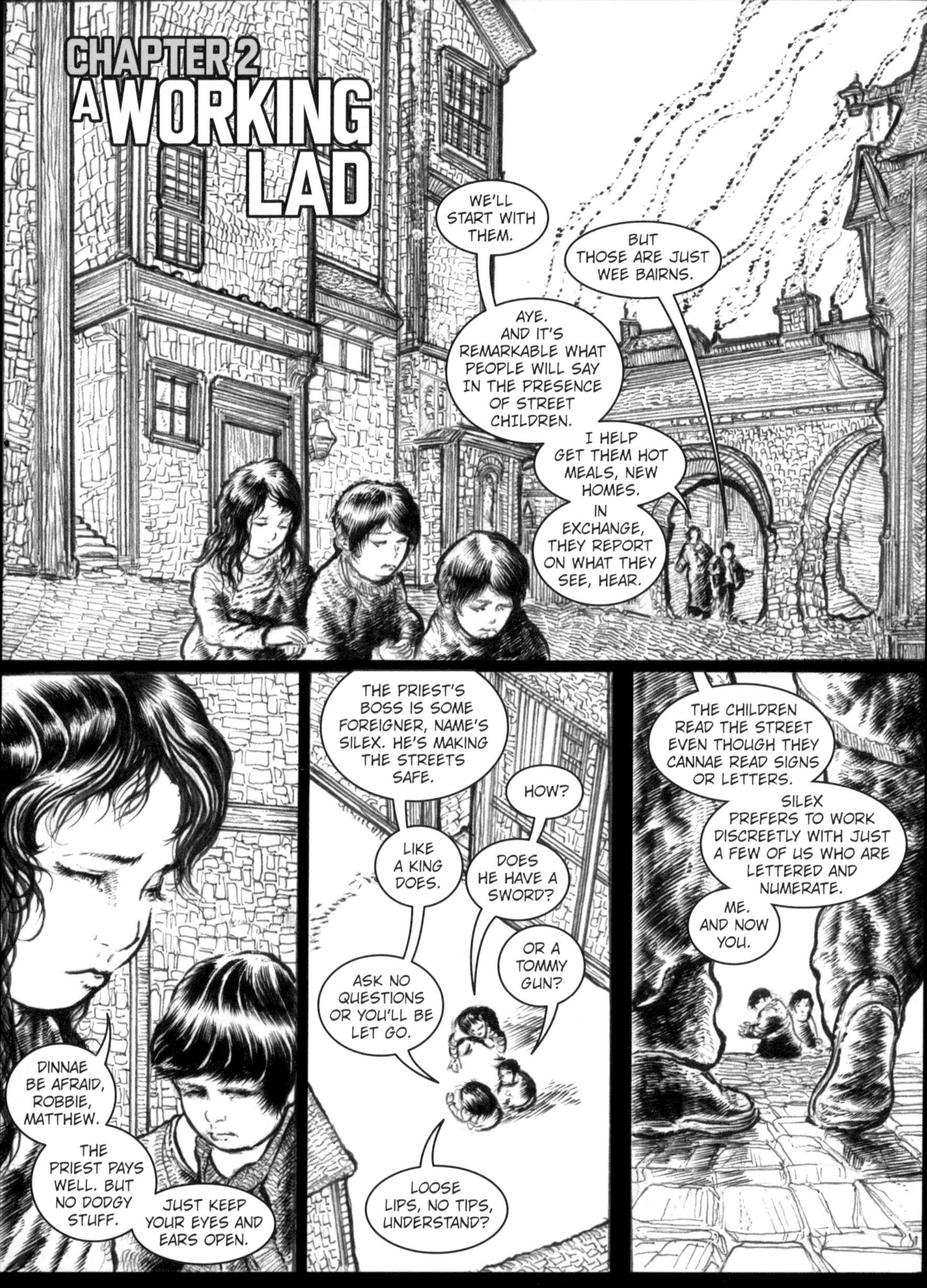
CHAPTER 2
A WORKING LAD
WE'LL START WITH THEM.
BUT THOSE ARE JUST WEE BAIRNS.
AYE. AND IT'S REMARKABLE WHAT PEOPLE WILL SAY IN THE PRESENCE OF STREET CHILDREN.
I HELP GET THEM HOT MEALS, NEW HOMES.
IN EXCHANGE, THEY REPORT ON WHAT THEY SEE, HEAR.
DINNAE BE AFRAID, ROBBIE, MATTHEW.
THE PRIEST PAYS WELL. BUT NO DODGY STUFF.
JUST KEEP YOUR EYES AND EARS OPEN.
THE PRIEST'S BOSS IS SOME FOREIGNER, NAME'S SILEX. HE'S MAKING THE STREETS SAFE.
HOW?
LIKE A KING DOES.
DOES HE HAVE A SWORD?
OR A TOMMY GUN?
ASK NO QUESTIONS OR YOU'LL BE LET GO.
LOOSE LIPS, NO TIPS, UNDERSTAND?
THE CHILDREN READ THE STREET EVEN THOUGH THEY CANNAE READ SIGNS OR LETTERS.
SILEX PREFERS TO WORK DISCREETLY WITH JUST A FEW OF US WHO ARE LETTERED AND NUMERATE.
ME. AND NOW YOU.

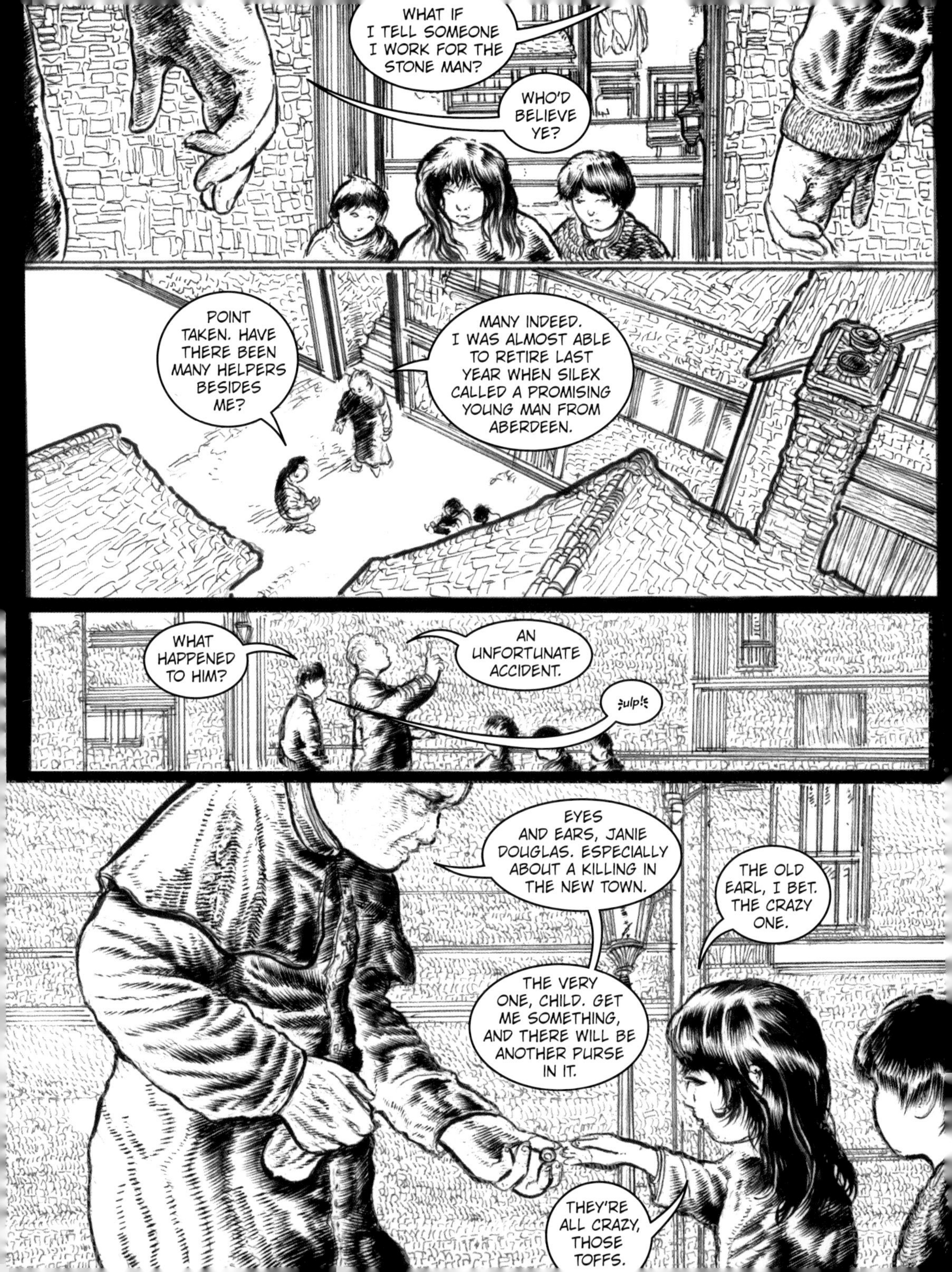
WHAT IF I TELL SOMEONE I WORK FOR THE STONE MAN?
WHO'D BELIEVE YE?
POINT TAKEN. HAVE THERE BEEN MANY HELPERS BESIDES ME?
MANY INDEED. I WAS ALMOST ABLE TO RETIRE LAST YEAR WHEN SILEX CALLED A PROMISING YOUNG MAN FROM ABERDEEN.
WHAT HAPPENED TO HIM?
AN UNFORTUNATE ACCIDENT.
ulp!
EYES AND EARS, JANIE DOUGLAS. ESPECIALLY ABOUT A KILLING IN THE NEW TOWN.
THE OLD EARL, I BET. THE CRAZY ONE.
THE VERY ONE, CHILD. GET ME SOMETHING, AND THERE WILL BE ANOTHER PURSE IN IT.
THEY'RE ALL CRAZY, THOSE TOFFS.

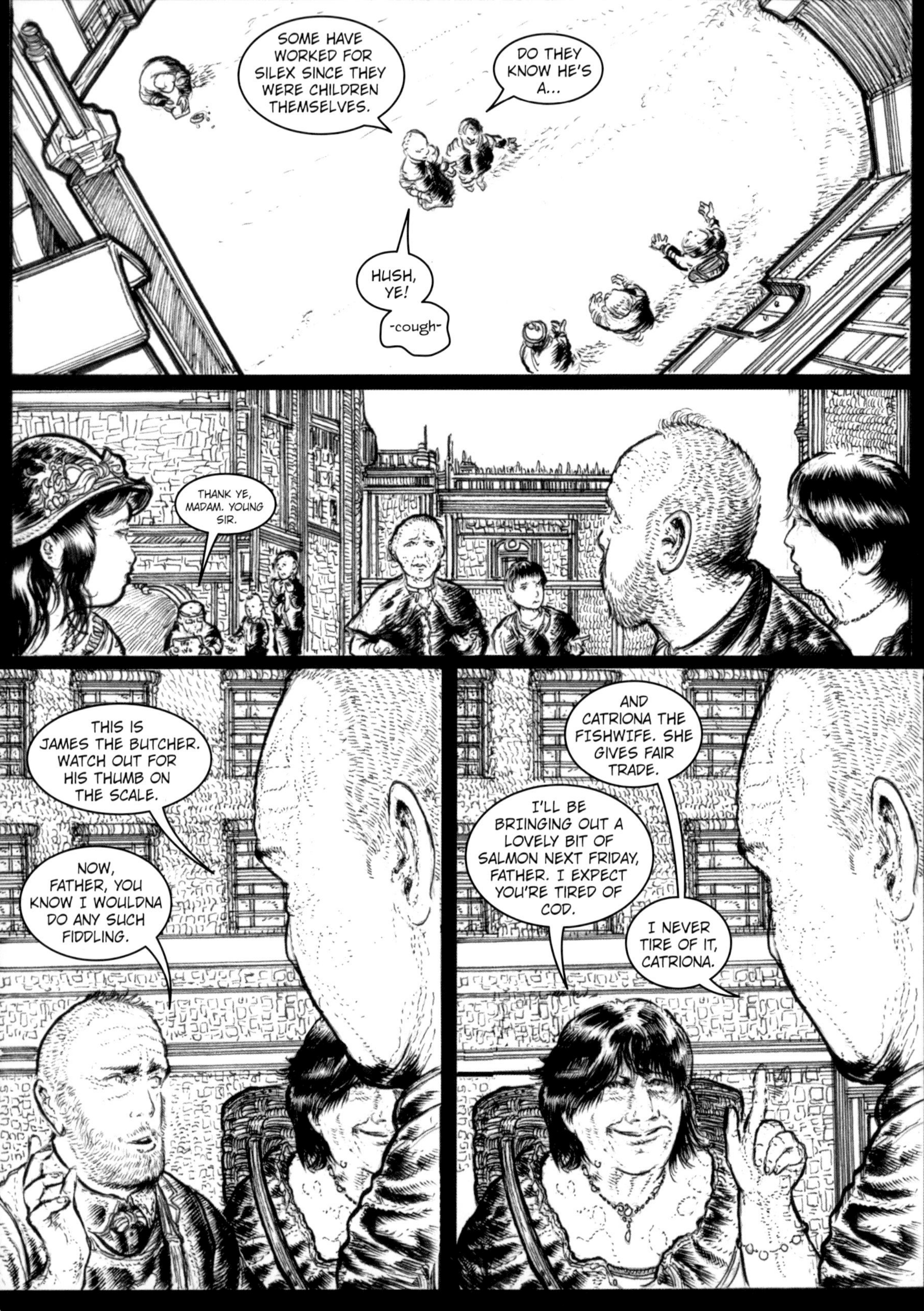
SOME HAVE WORKED FOR SILEX SINCE THEY WERE CHILDREN THEMSELVES.
DO THEY KNOW HE'S A...
HUSH, YE!
-cough-
THANK YE, MADAM. YOUNG SIR.
THIS IS JAMES THE BUTCHER. WATCH OUT FOR HIS THUMB ON THE SCALE.
NOW, FATHER, YOU KNOW I WOULDNA DO ANY SUCH FIDDLING.
AND CATRIONA THE FISHWIFE. SHE GIVES FAIR TRADE.
I'LL BE BRINGING OUT A LOVELY BIT OF SALMON NEXT FRIDAY, FATHER. I EXPECT YOU'RE TIRED OF COD.
I NEVER TIRE OF IT, CATRIONA.

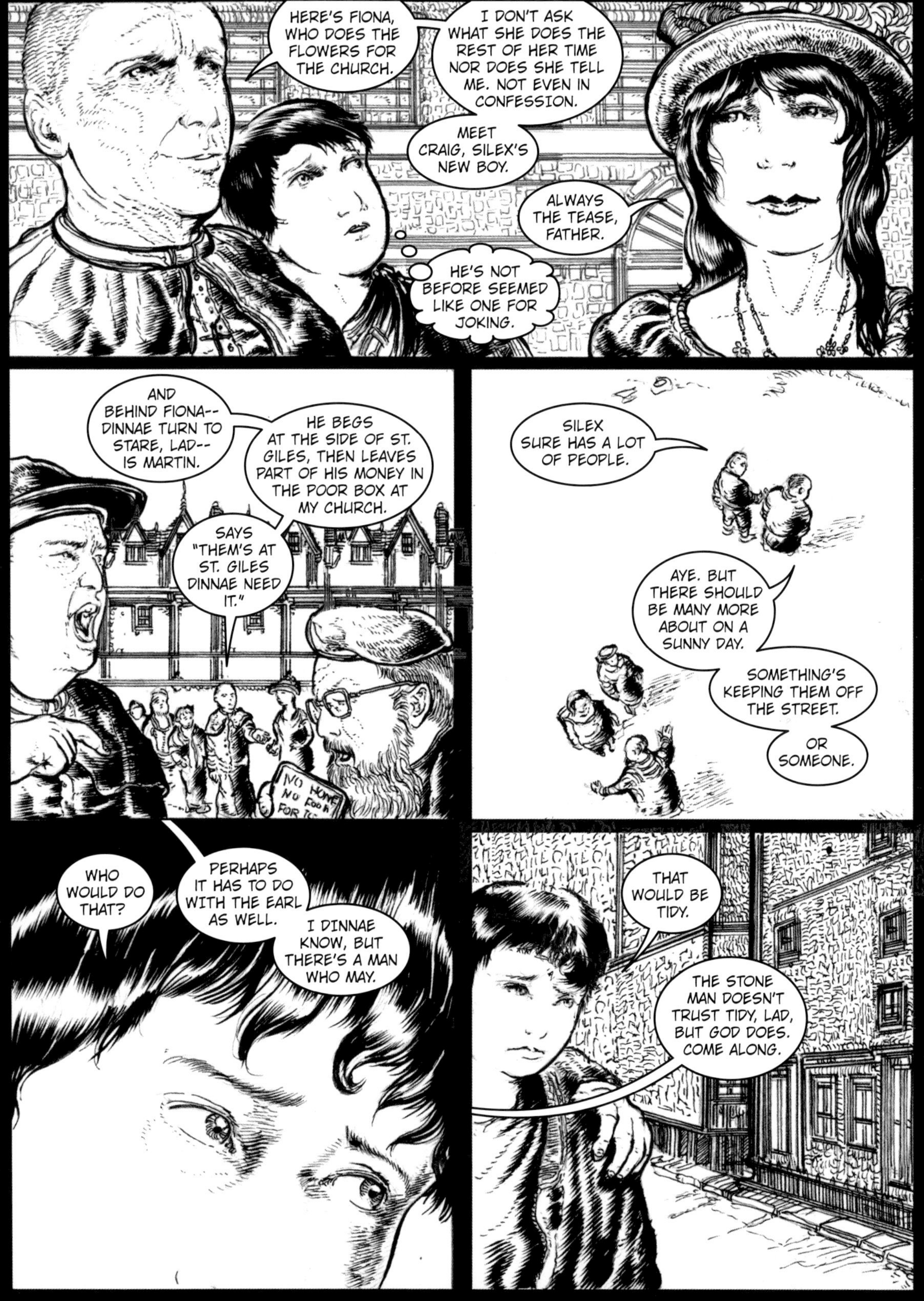
HERE'S FIONA, WHO DOES THE FLOWERS FOR THE CHURCH.
I DON'T ASK WHAT SHE DOES THE REST OF HER TIME NOR DOES SHE TELL ME. NOT EVEN IN CONFESSION.
MEET CRAIG, SILEX'S NEW BOY.
ALWAYS THE TEASE, FATHER.
HE'S NOT BEFORE SEEMED LIKE ONE FOR JOKING.
AND BEHIND FIONA-- DINNAE TURN TO STARE, LAD-- IS MARTIN.
HE BEGS AT THE SIDE OF ST. GILES, THEN LEAVES PART OF HIS MONEY IN THE POOR BOX AT MY CHURCH.
SAYS "THEM'S AT ST. GILES DINNAE NEED IT."
SILEX SURE HAS A LOT OF PEOPLE.
AYE. BUT THERE SHOULD BE MANY MORE ABOUT ON A SUNNY DAY.
SOMETHING'S KEEPING THEM OFF THE STREET.
OR SOMEONE.
WHO WOULD DO THAT?
PERHAPS IT HAS TO DO WITH THE EARL AS WELL.
I DINNAE KNOW, BUT THERE'S A MAN WHO MAY.
THAT WOULD BE TIDY.
THE STONE MAN DOESN'T TRUST TIDY, LAD, BUT GOD DOES. COME ALONG.

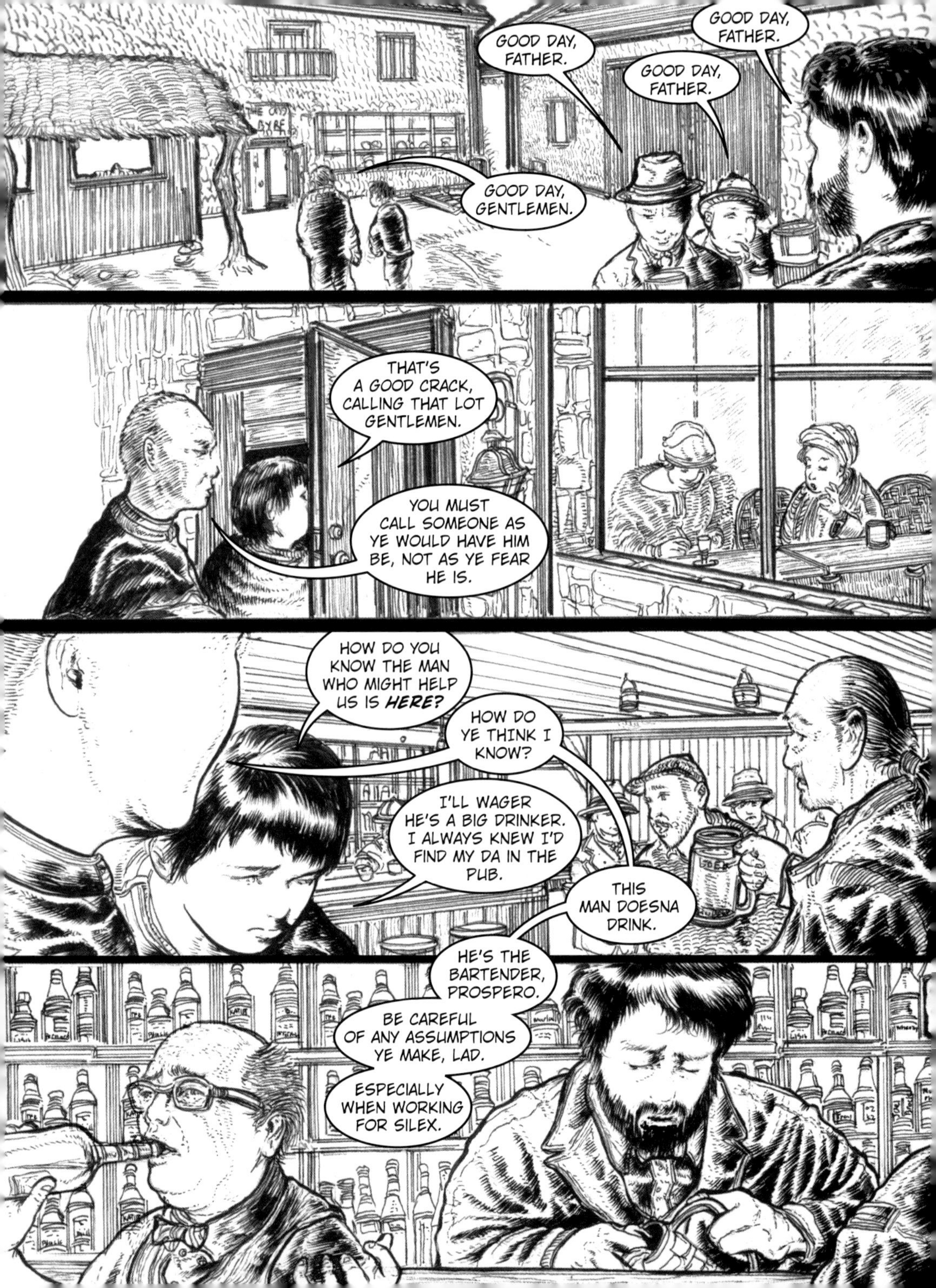
GOOD DAY, FATHER.
GOOD DAY, FATHER.
GOOD DAY, FATHER.
GOOD DAY, GENTLEMEN.
THAT'S A GOOD CRACK, CALLING THAT LOT GENTLEMEN.
YOU MUST CALL SOMEONE AS YE WOULD HAVE HIM BE, NOT AS YE FEAR HE IS.
HOW DO YOU KNOW THE MAN WHO MIGHT HELP US IS *HERE?*
HOW DO YE THINK I KNOW?
I'LL WAGER HE'S A BIG DRINKER. I ALWAYS KNEW I'D FIND MY DA IN THE PUB.
THIS MAN DOESNA DRINK.
HE'S THE BARTENDER, PROSPERO.
BE CAREFUL OF ANY ASSUMPTIONS YE MAKE, LAD.
ESPECIALLY WHEN WORKING FOR SILEX.

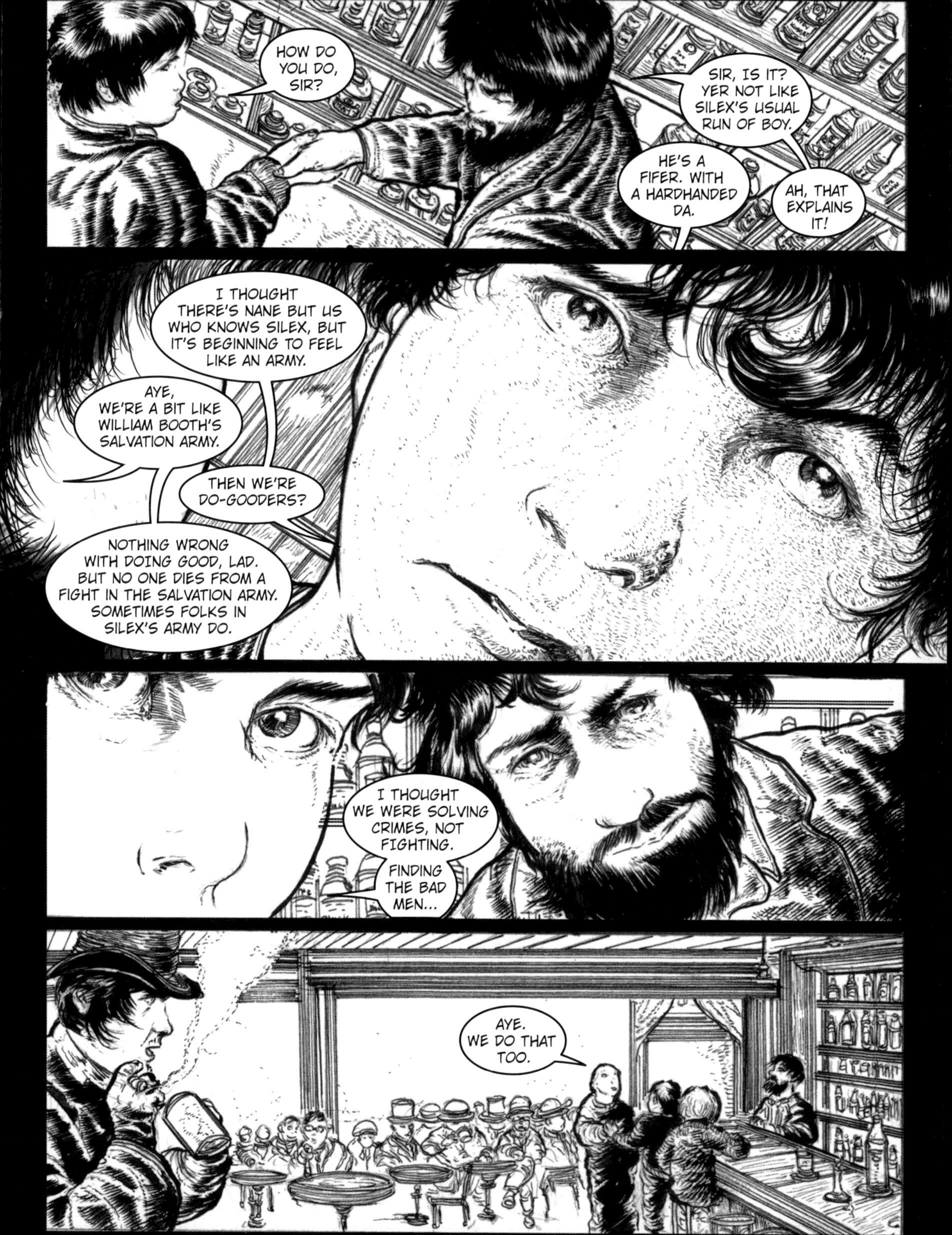
HOW DO YOU DO, SIR?
SIR, IS IT? YER NOT LIKE SILEX'S USUAL RUN OF BOY.
HE'S A FIFER. WITH A HARDHANDED DA.
AH, THAT EXPLAINS IT!
I THOUGHT THERE'S NANE BUT US WHO KNOWS SILEX, BUT IT'S BEGINNING TO FEEL LIKE AN ARMY.
AYE, WE'RE A BIT LIKE WILLIAM BOOTH'S SALVATION ARMY.
THEN WE'RE DO-GOODERS?
NOTHING WRONG WITH DOING GOOD, LAD. BUT NO ONE DIES FROM A FIGHT IN THE SALVATION ARMY. SOMETIMES FOLKS IN SILEX'S ARMY DO.
I THOUGHT WE WERE SOLVING CRIMES, NOT FIGHTING.
FINDING THE BAD MEN...
AYE. WE DO THAT TOO.

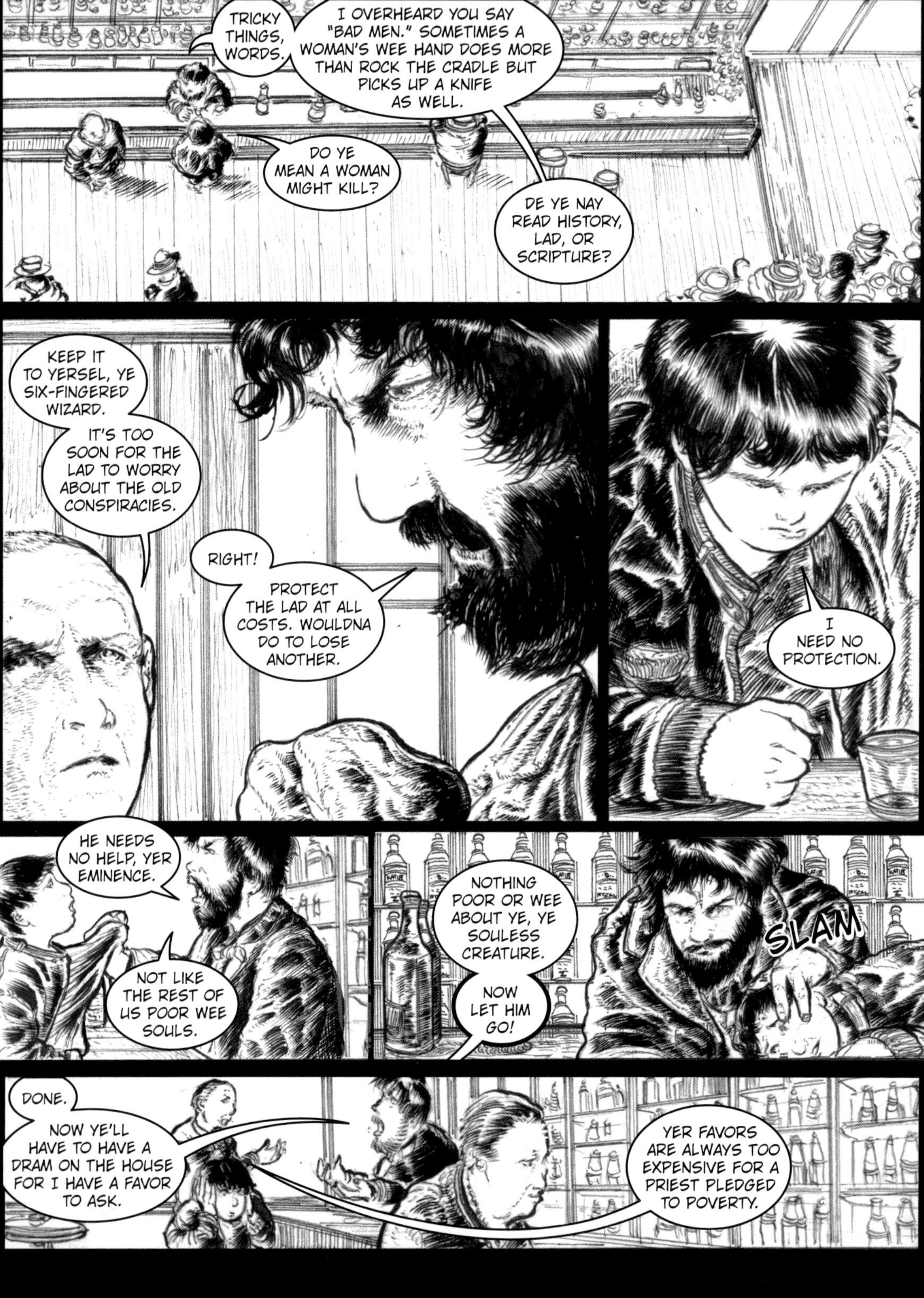

TRICKY THINGS, WORDS.
I OVERHEARD YOU SAY "BAD MEN." SOMETIMES A WOMAN'S WEE HAND DOES MORE THAN ROCK THE CRADLE BUT PICKS UP A KNIFE AS WELL.
DO YE MEAN A WOMAN MIGHT KILL?
DE YE NAY READ HISTORY, LAD, OR SCRIPTURE?
KEEP IT TO YERSEL, YE SIX-FINGERED WIZARD.
IT'S TOO SOON FOR THE LAD TO WORRY ABOUT THE OLD CONSPIRACIES.
RIGHT!
PROTECT THE LAD AT ALL COSTS. WOULDNA DO TO LOSE ANOTHER.
I NEED NO PROTECTION.
HE NEEDS NO HELP, YER EMINENCE.
NOT LIKE THE REST OF US POOR WEE SOULS.
NOTHING POOR OR WEE ABOUT YE, YE SOULESS CREATURE.
NOW LET HIM GO!
SLAM
DONE.
NOW YE'LL HAVE TO HAVE A DRAM ON THE HOUSE FOR I HAVE A FAVOR TO ASK.
YER FAVORS ARE ALWAYS TOO EXPENSIVE FOR A PRIEST PLEDGED TO POVERTY.

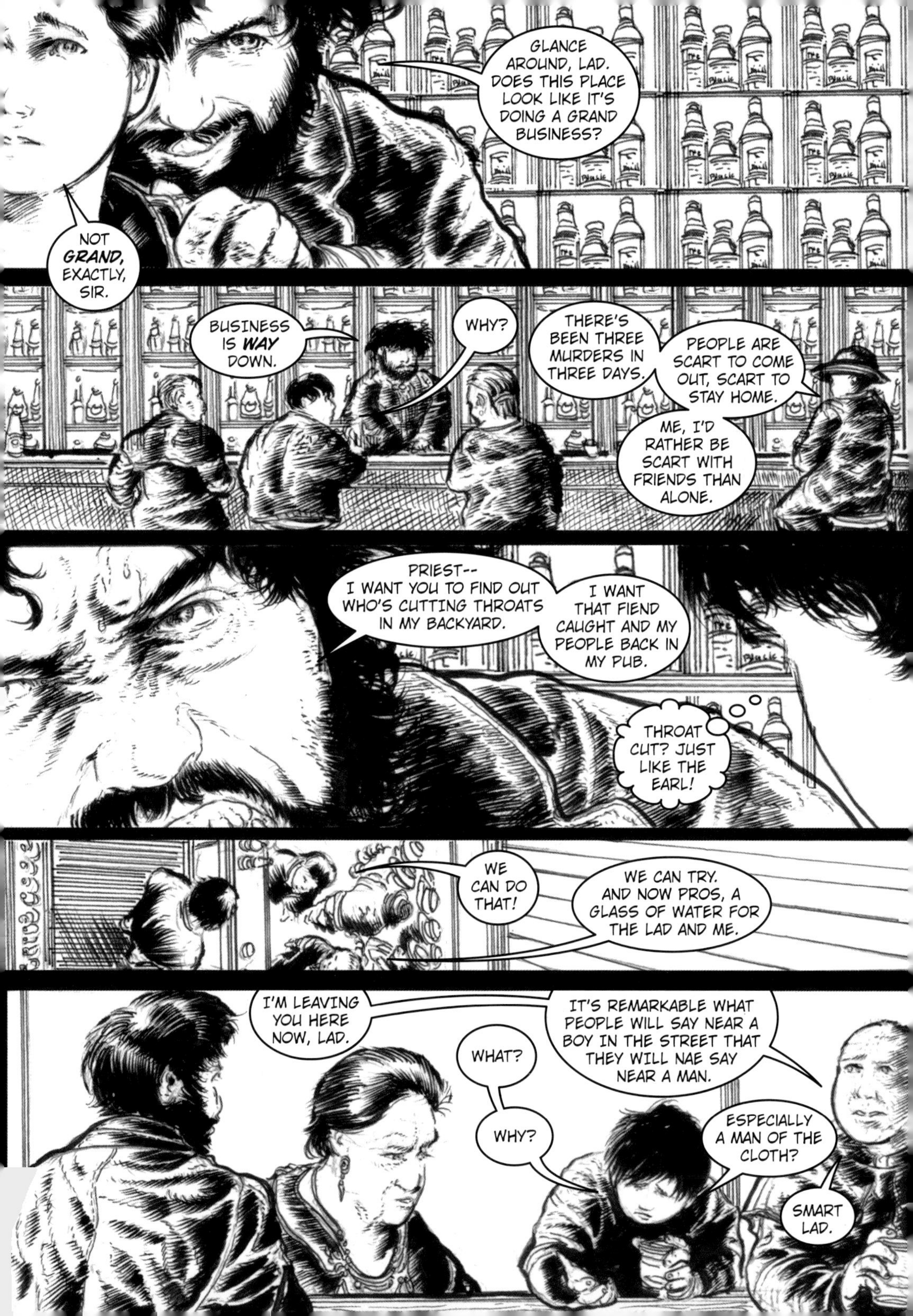
GLANCE AROUND, LAD. DOES THIS PLACE LOOK LIKE IT'S DOING A GRAND BUSINESS?
NOT **GRAND,** EXACTLY, SIR.
BUSINESS IS **WAY** DOWN.
WHY?
THERE'S BEEN THREE MURDERS IN THREE DAYS.
PEOPLE ARE SCART TO COME OUT, SCART TO STAY HOME.
ME, I'D RATHER BE SCART WITH FRIENDS THAN ALONE.
PRIEST-- I WANT YOU TO FIND OUT WHO'S CUTTING THROATS IN MY BACKYARD.
I WANT THAT FIEND CAUGHT AND MY PEOPLE BACK IN MY PUB.
THROAT CUT? JUST LIKE THE EARL!
WE CAN DO THAT!
WE CAN TRY. AND NOW PROS, A GLASS OF WATER FOR THE LAD AND ME.
I'M LEAVING YOU HERE NOW, LAD.
WHAT?
IT'S REMARKABLE WHAT PEOPLE WILL SAY NEAR A BOY IN THE STREET THAT THEY WILL NAE SAY NEAR A MAN.
WHY?
ESPECIALLY A MAN OF THE CLOTH?
SMART LAD.

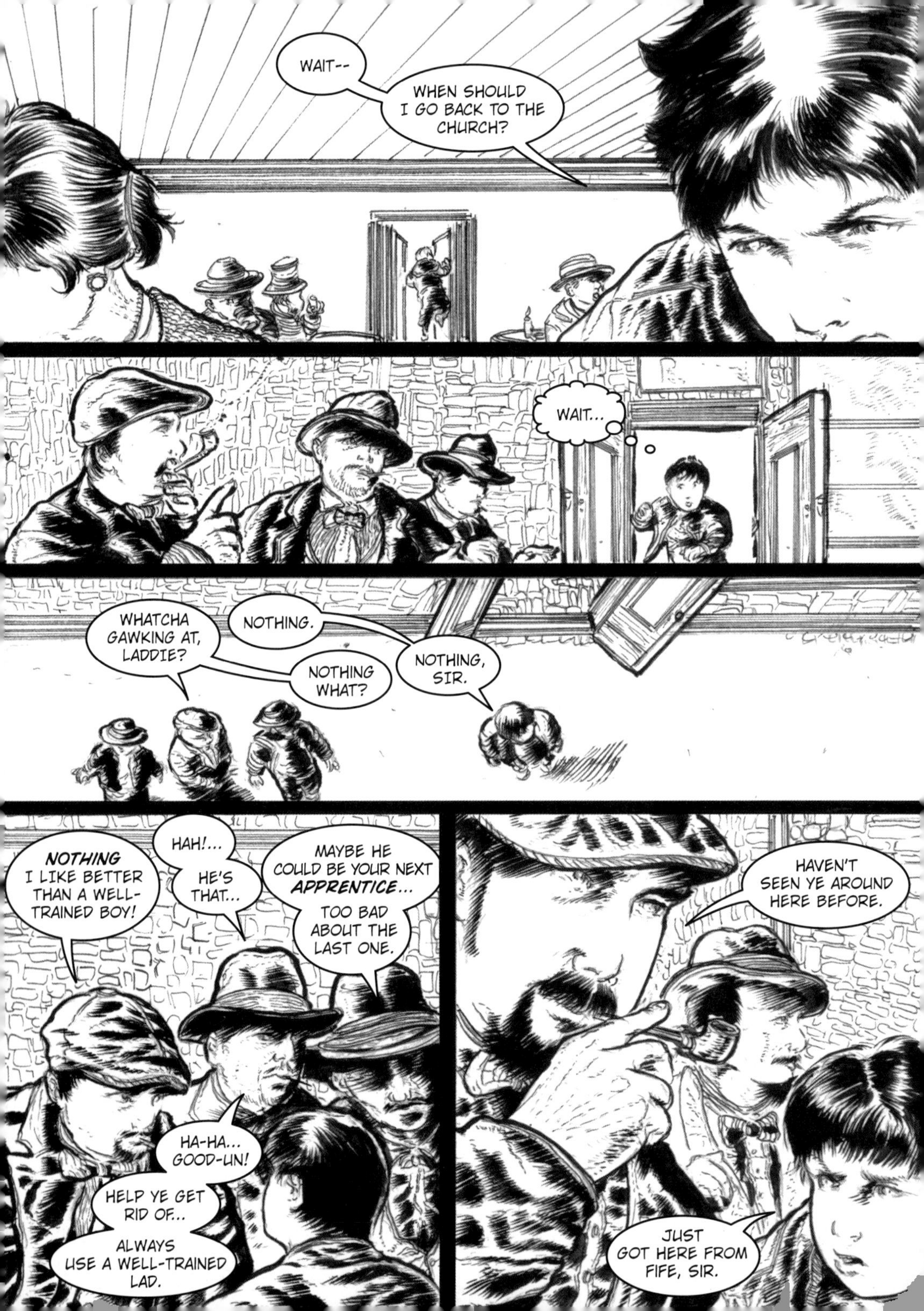
WAIT--
WHEN SHOULD I GO BACK TO THE CHURCH?
WAIT...
WHATCHA GAWKING AT, LADDIE?
NOTHING.
NOTHING WHAT?
NOTHING, SIR.
NOTHING I LIKE BETTER THAN A WELL-TRAINED BOY!
HAH!...
HE'S THAT...
MAYBE HE COULD BE YOUR NEXT APPRENTICE...
TOO BAD ABOUT THE LAST ONE.
HA-HA... GOOD-UN!
HELP YE GET RID OF...
ALWAYS USE A WELL-TRAINED LAD.
HAVEN'T SEEN YE AROUND HERE BEFORE.
JUST GOT HERE FROM FIFE, SIR.

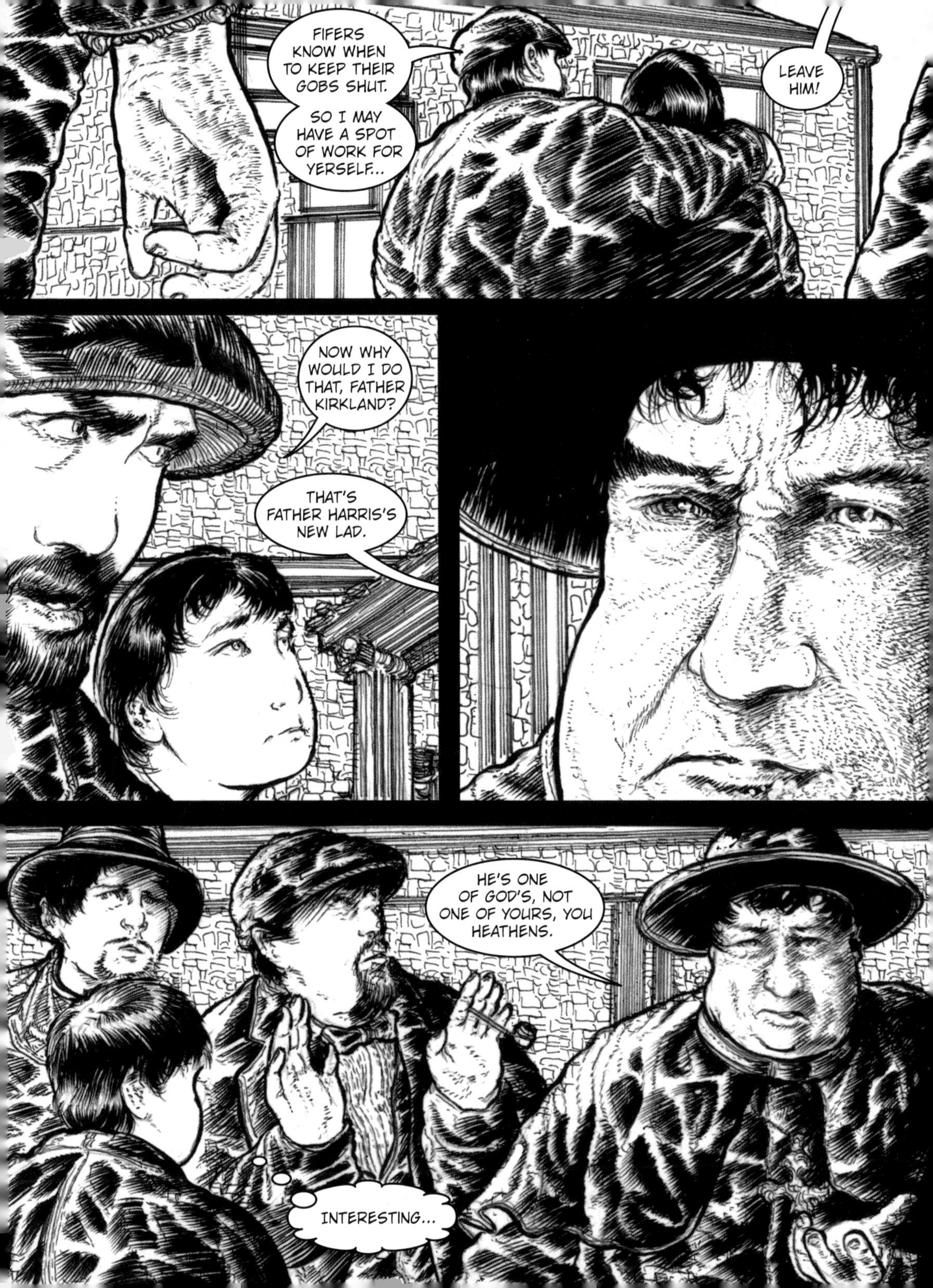
FIFERS KNOW WHEN TO KEEP THEIR GOBS SHUT.
SO I MAY HAVE A SPOT OF WORK FOR YERSELF...
LEAVE HIM!
NOW WHY WOULD I DO THAT, FATHER KIRKLAND?
THAT'S FATHER HARRIS'S NEW LAD.
HE'S ONE OF GOD'S, NOT ONE OF YOURS, YOU HEATHENS.
INTERESTING...

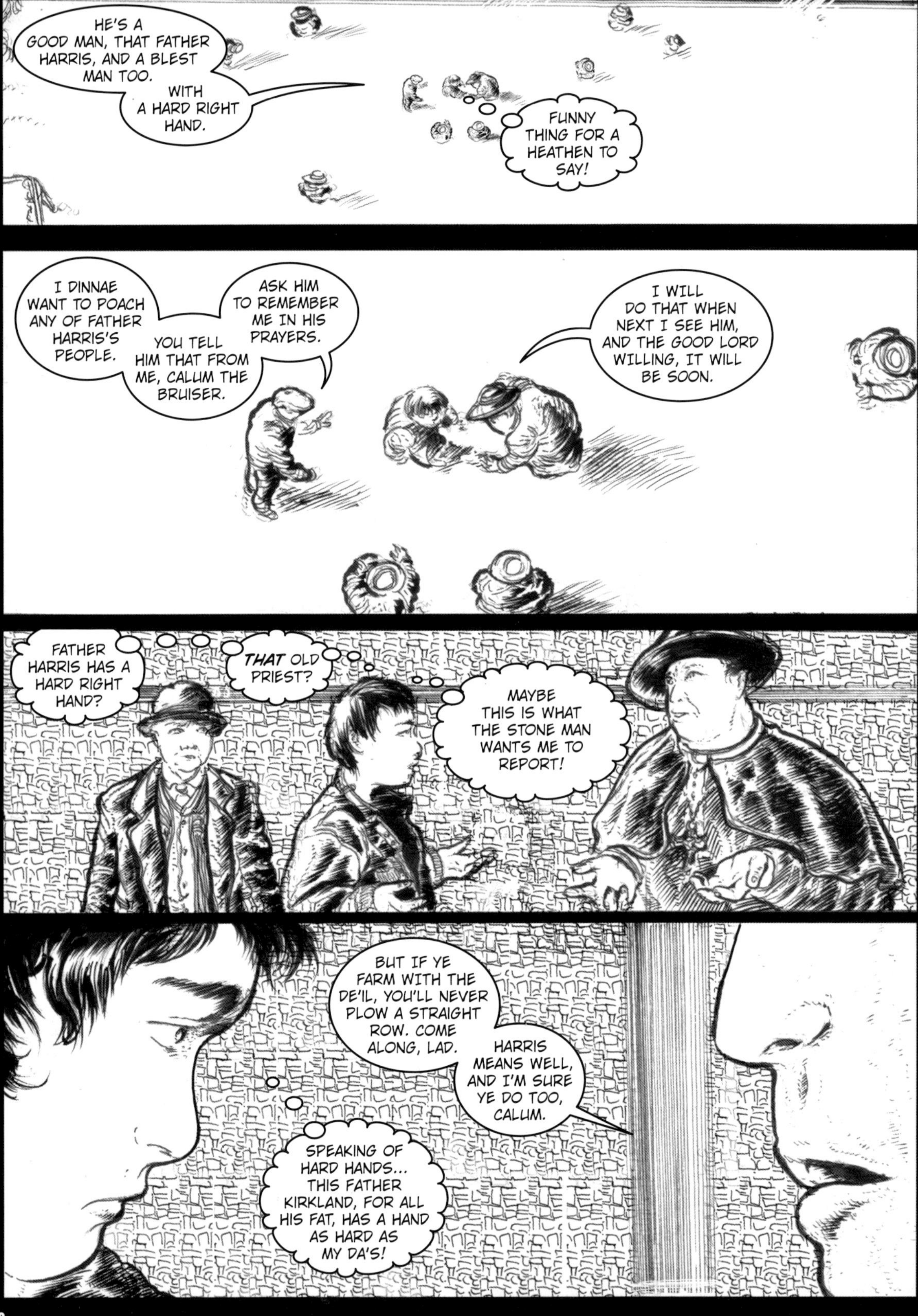
HE'S A GOOD MAN, THAT FATHER HARRIS, AND A BLEST MAN TOO.
WITH A HARD RIGHT HAND.
FUNNY THING FOR A HEATHEN TO SAY!
I DINNAE WANT TO POACH ANY OF FATHER HARRIS'S PEOPLE.
YOU TELL HIM THAT FROM ME, CALUM THE BRUISER.
ASK HIM TO REMEMBER ME IN HIS PRAYERS.
I WILL DO THAT WHEN NEXT I SEE HIM, AND THE GOOD LORD WILLING, IT WILL BE SOON.
FATHER HARRIS HAS A HARD RIGHT HAND?
THAT OLD PRIEST?
MAYBE THIS IS WHAT THE STONE MAN WANTS ME TO REPORT!
BUT IF YE FARM WITH THE DE'IL, YOU'LL NEVER PLOW A STRAIGHT ROW. COME ALONG, LAD.
HARRIS MEANS WELL, AND I'M SURE YE DO TOO, CALUM.
SPEAKING OF HARD HANDS... THIS FATHER KIRKLAND, FOR ALL HIS FAT, HAS A HAND AS HARD AS MY DA'S!

CHAPTER 3
WORKING THE EARL'S CASE

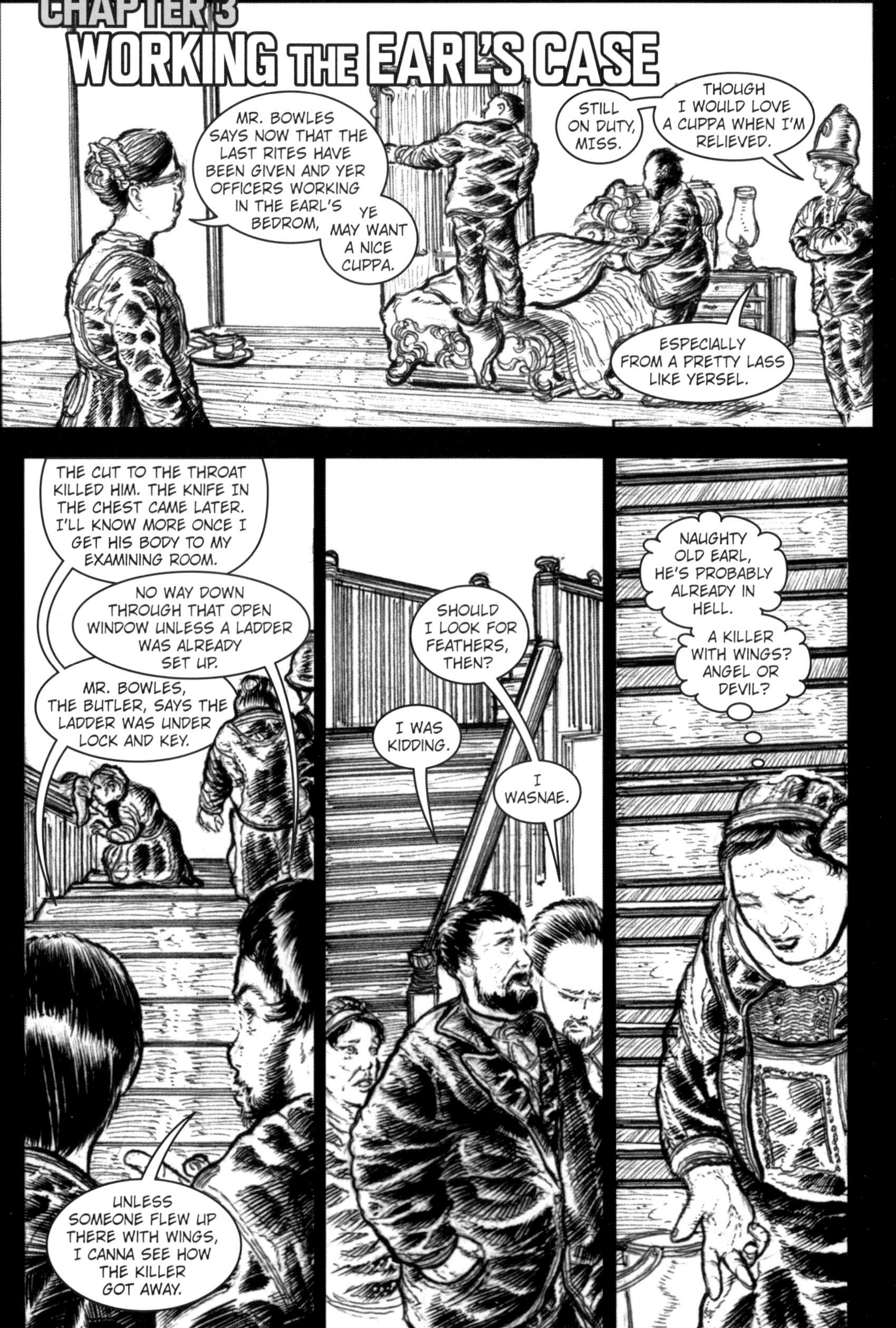
MR. BOWLES SAYS NOW THAT THE LAST RITES HAVE BEEN GIVEN AND YER OFFICERS WORKING IN THE EARL'S BEDROM,
YE MAY WANT A NICE CUPPA.
STILL ON DUTY, MISS.
THOUGH I WOULD LOVE A CUPPA WHEN I'M RELIEVED.
ESPECIALLY FROM A PRETTY LASS LIKE YERSEL.
THE CUT TO THE THROAT KILLED HIM. THE KNIFE IN THE CHEST CAME LATER. I'LL KNOW MORE ONCE I GET HIS BODY TO MY EXAMINING ROOM.
NO WAY DOWN THROUGH THAT OPEN WINDOW UNLESS A LADDER WAS ALREADY SET UP.
MR. BOWLES, THE BUTLER, SAYS THE LADDER WAS UNDER LOCK AND KEY.
UNLESS SOMEONE FLEW UP THERE WITH WINGS, I CANNA SEE HOW THE KILLER GOT AWAY.
SHOULD I LOOK FOR FEATHERS, THEN?
I WAS KIDDING.
I WASNAE.
NAUGHTY OLD EARL, HE'S PROBABLY ALREADY IN HELL.
A KILLER WITH WINGS? ANGEL OR DEVIL?

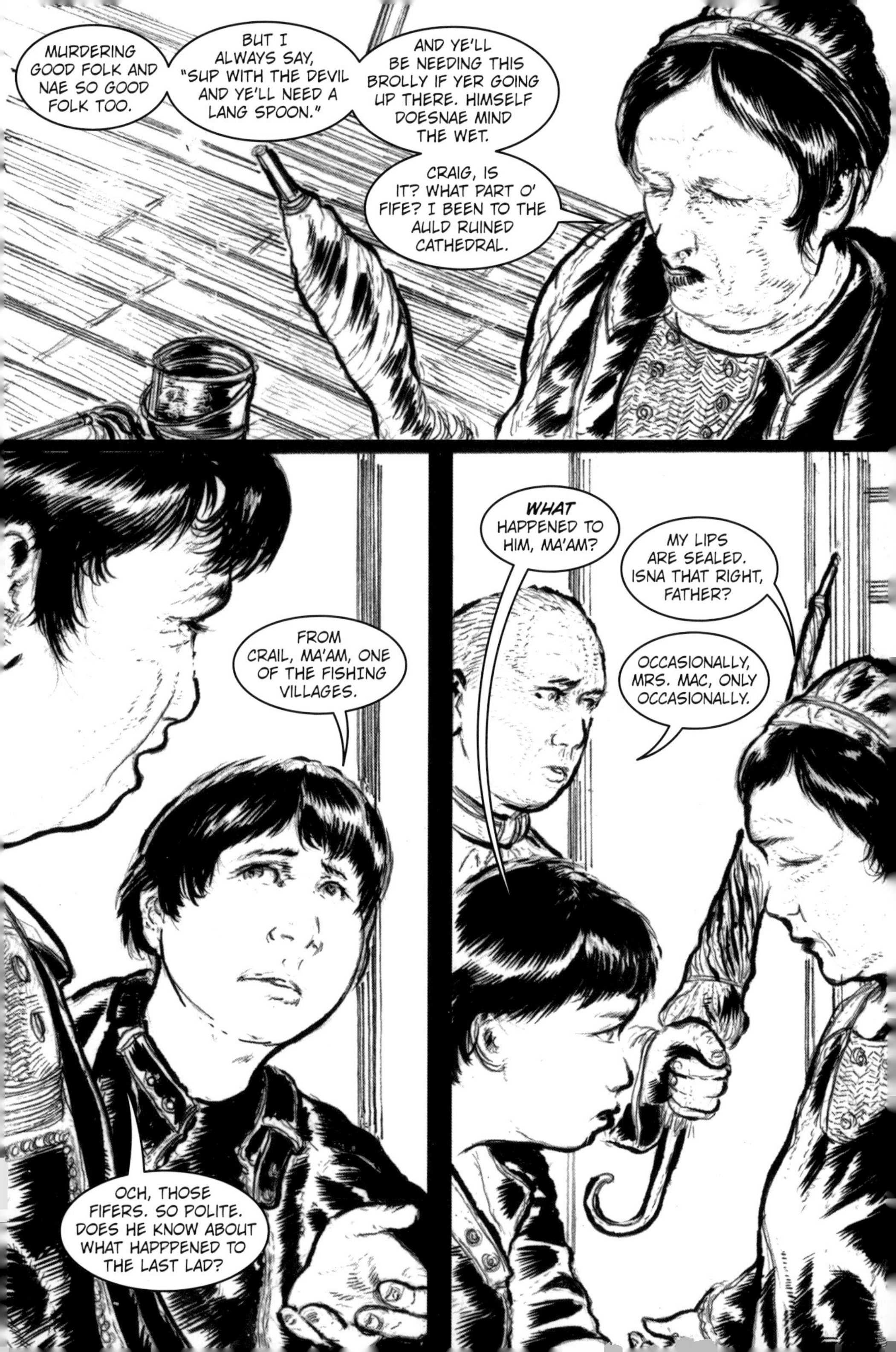
MURDERING GOOD FOLK AND NAE SO GOOD FOLK TOO.
BUT I ALWAYS SAY, "SUP WITH THE DEVIL AND YE'LL NEED A LANG SPOON."
AND YE'LL BE NEEDING THIS BROLLY IF YER GOING UP THERE. HIMSELF DOESNAE MIND THE WET.
CRAIG, IS IT? WHAT PART O' FIFE? I BEEN TO THE AULD RUINED CATHEDRAL.
FROM CRAIL, MA'AM, ONE OF THE FISHING VILLAGES.
OCH, THOSE FIFERS. SO POLITE. DOES HE KNOW ABOUT WHAT HAPPPENED TO THE LAST LAD?
WHAT HAPPENED TO HIM, MA'AM?
MY LIPS ARE SEALED. ISNA THAT RIGHT, FATHER?
OCCASIONALLY, MRS. MAC, ONLY OCCASIONALLY.

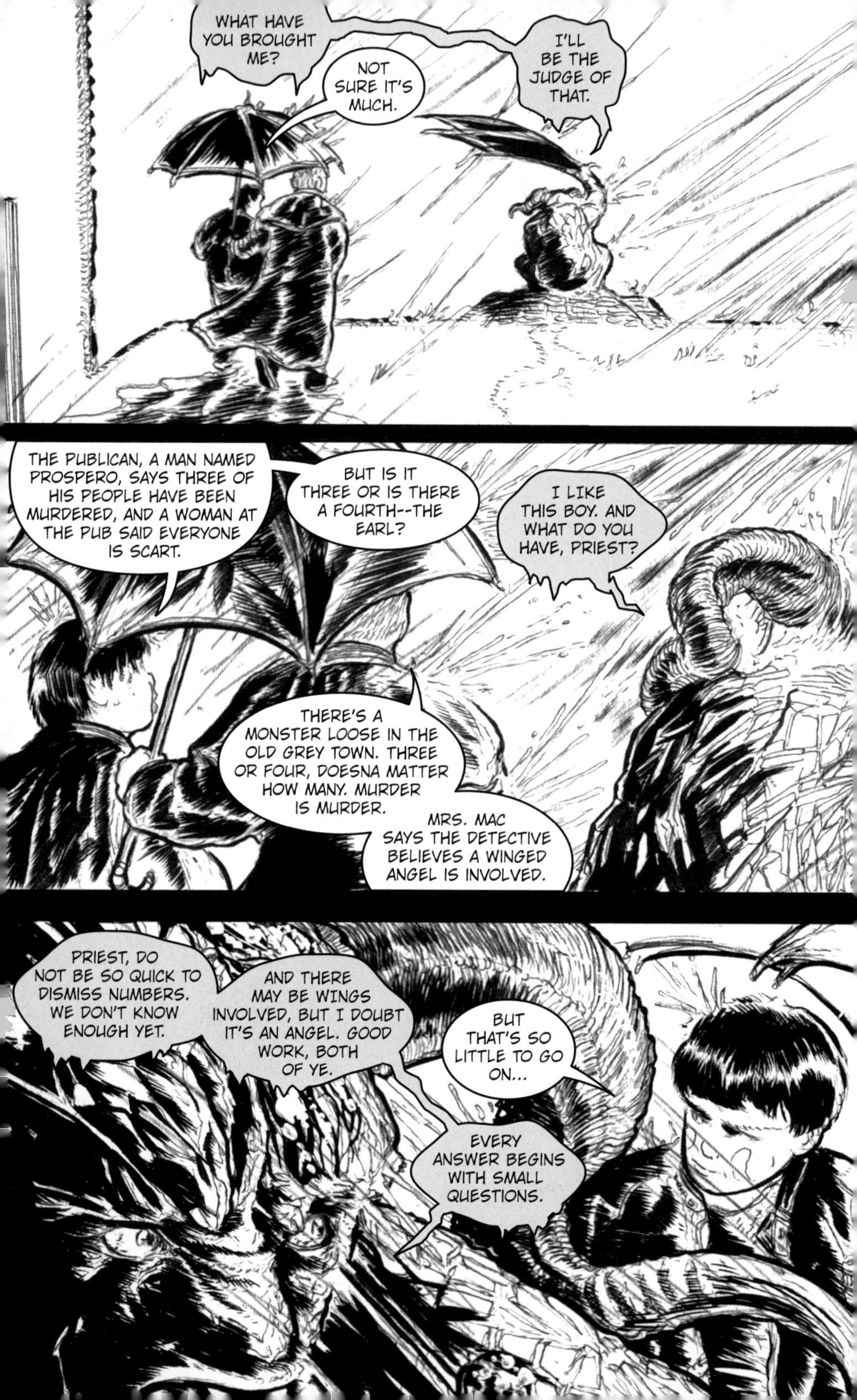
WHAT HAVE YOU BROUGHT ME?
NOT SURE IT'S MUCH.
I'LL BE THE JUDGE OF THAT.
THE PUBLICAN, A MAN NAMED PROSPERO, SAYS THREE OF HIS PEOPLE HAVE BEEN MURDERED, AND A WOMAN AT THE PUB SAID EVERYONE IS SCART.
BUT IS IT THREE OR IS THERE A FOURTH--THE EARL?
I LIKE THIS BOY. AND WHAT DO YOU HAVE, PRIEST?
THERE'S A MONSTER LOOSE IN THE OLD GREY TOWN. THREE OR FOUR, DOESNA MATTER HOW MANY. MURDER IS MURDER.
MRS. MAC SAYS THE DETECTIVE BELIEVES A WINGED ANGEL IS INVOLVED.
PRIEST, DO NOT BE SO QUICK TO DISMISS NUMBERS. WE DON'T KNOW ENOUGH YET.
AND THERE MAY BE WINGS INVOLVED, BUT I DOUBT IT'S AN ANGEL. GOOD WORK, BOTH OF YE.
BUT THAT'S SO LITTLE TO GO ON...
EVERY ANSWER BEGINS WITH SMALL QUESTIONS.

CHAPTER 4
CLUES FOR THE STONE MAN

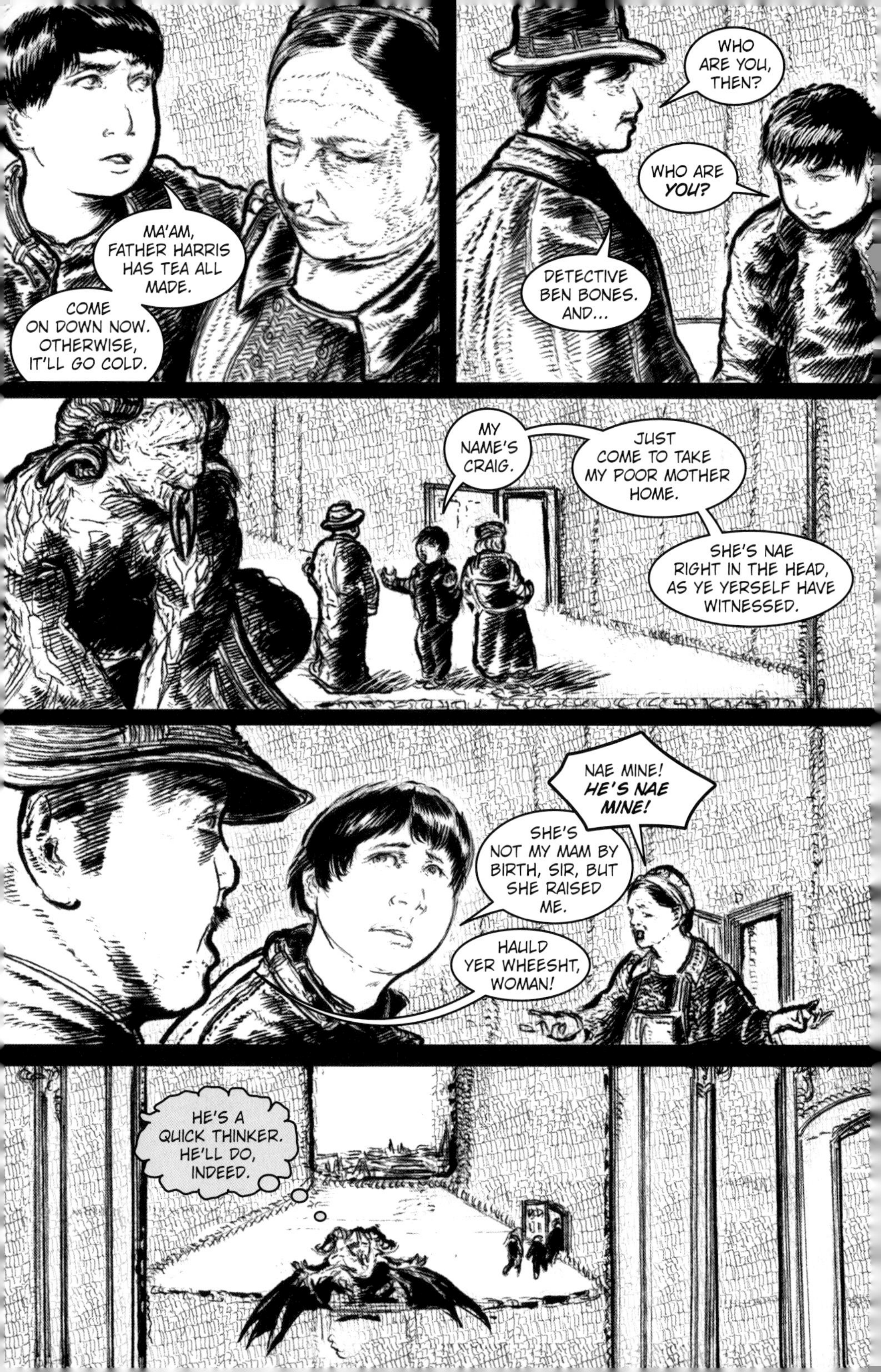
MA'AM, FATHER HARRIS HAS TEA ALL MADE.
COME ON DOWN NOW. OTHERWISE, IT'LL GO COLD.
WHO ARE YOU, THEN?
WHO ARE *YOU?*
DETECTIVE BEN BONES. AND...
MY NAME'S CRAIG.
JUST COME TO TAKE MY POOR MOTHER HOME.
SHE'S NAE RIGHT IN THE HEAD, AS YE YERSELF HAVE WITNESSED.
NAE MINE! ***HE'S NAE MINE!***
SHE'S NOT MY MAM BY BIRTH, SIR, BUT SHE RAISED ME.
HAULD YER WHEESHT, WOMAN!
HE'S A QUICK THINKER. HE'LL DO, INDEED.

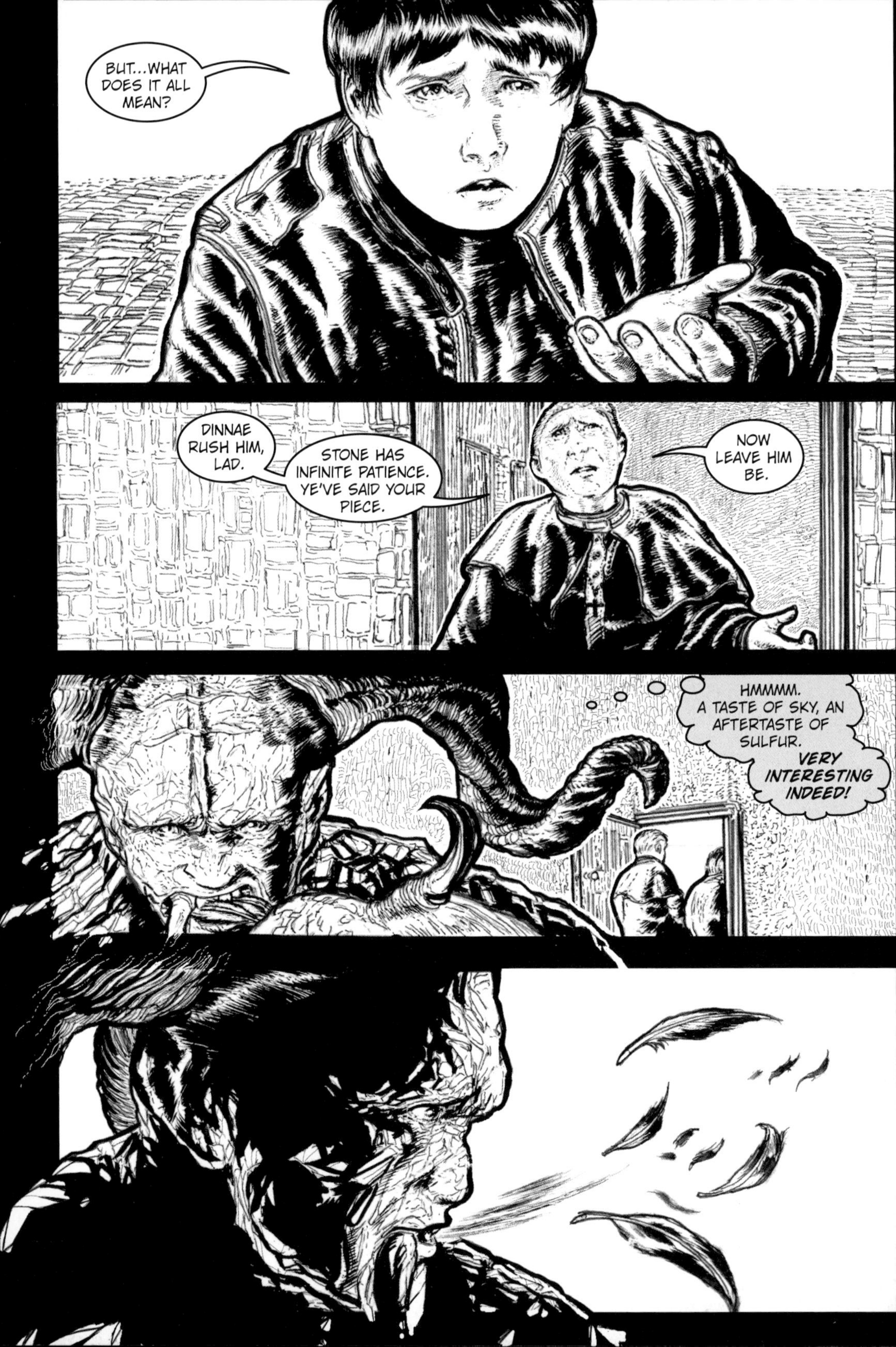
BUT...WHAT DOES IT ALL MEAN?
DINNAE RUSH HIM, LAD.
STONE HAS INFINITE PATIENCE. YE'VE SAID YOUR PIECE.
NOW LEAVE HIM BE.
HMMMM. A TASTE OF SKY, AN AFTERTASTE OF SULFUR.
VERY INTERESTING INDEED!

CHAPTER 5
THE NEXT DAY: DISCOVERIES

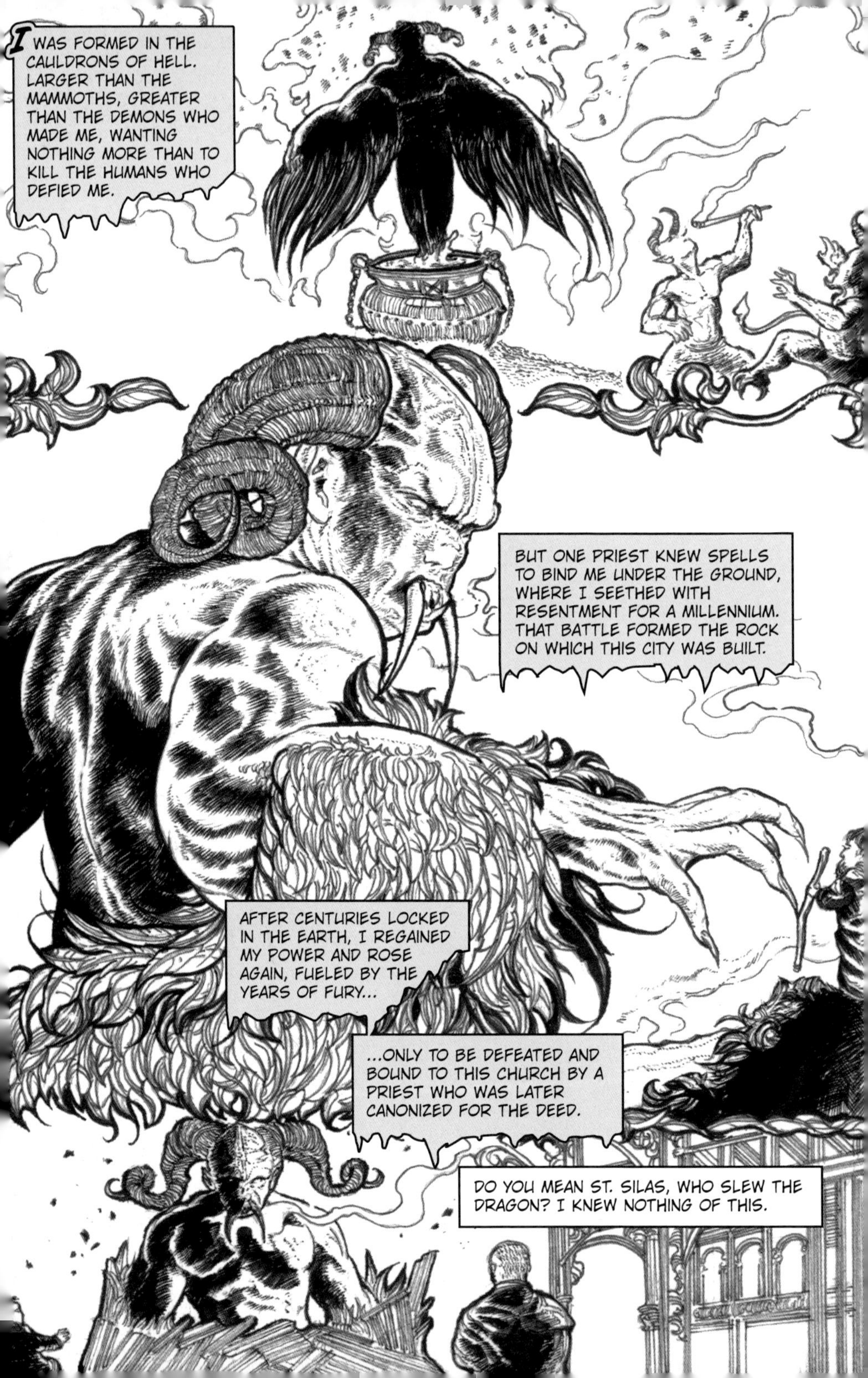
I WAS FORMED IN THE CAULDRONS OF HELL. LARGER THAN THE MAMMOTHS, GREATER THAN THE DEMONS WHO MADE ME, WANTING NOTHING MORE THAN TO KILL THE HUMANS WHO DEFIED ME.
BUT ONE PRIEST KNEW SPELLS TO BIND ME UNDER THE GROUND, WHERE I SEETHED WITH RESENTMENT FOR A MILLENNIUM. THAT BATTLE FORMED THE ROCK ON WHICH THIS CITY WAS BUILT.
AFTER CENTURIES LOCKED IN THE EARTH, I REGAINED MY POWER AND ROSE AGAIN, FUELED BY THE YEARS OF FURY...
...ONLY TO BE DEFEATED AND BOUND TO THIS CHURCH BY A PRIEST WHO WAS LATER CANONIZED FOR THE DEED.
DO YOU MEAN ST. SILAS, WHO SLEW THE DRAGON? I KNEW NOTHING OF THIS.

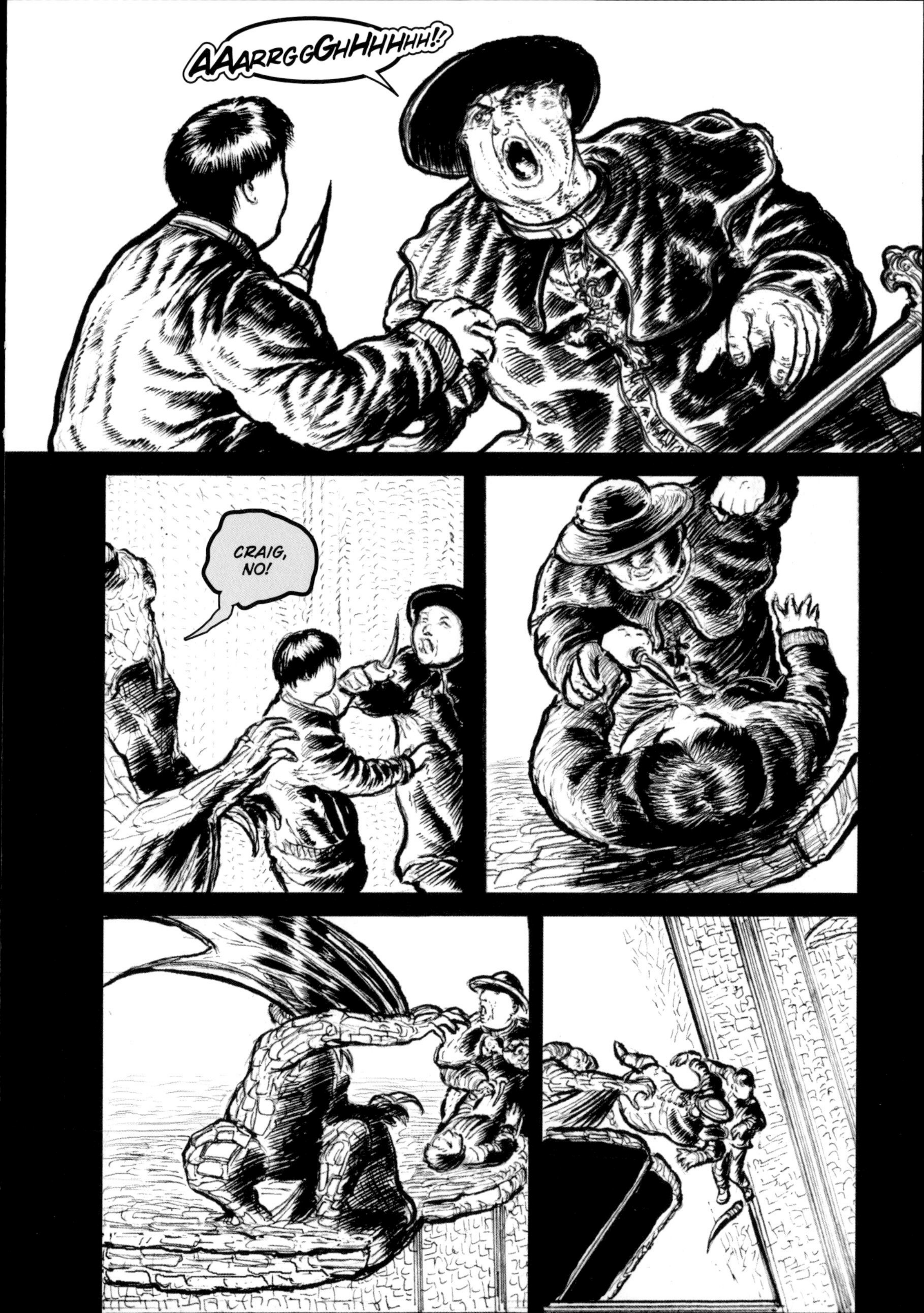
AAARRGGGHHHHHH!!
CRAIG, NO!

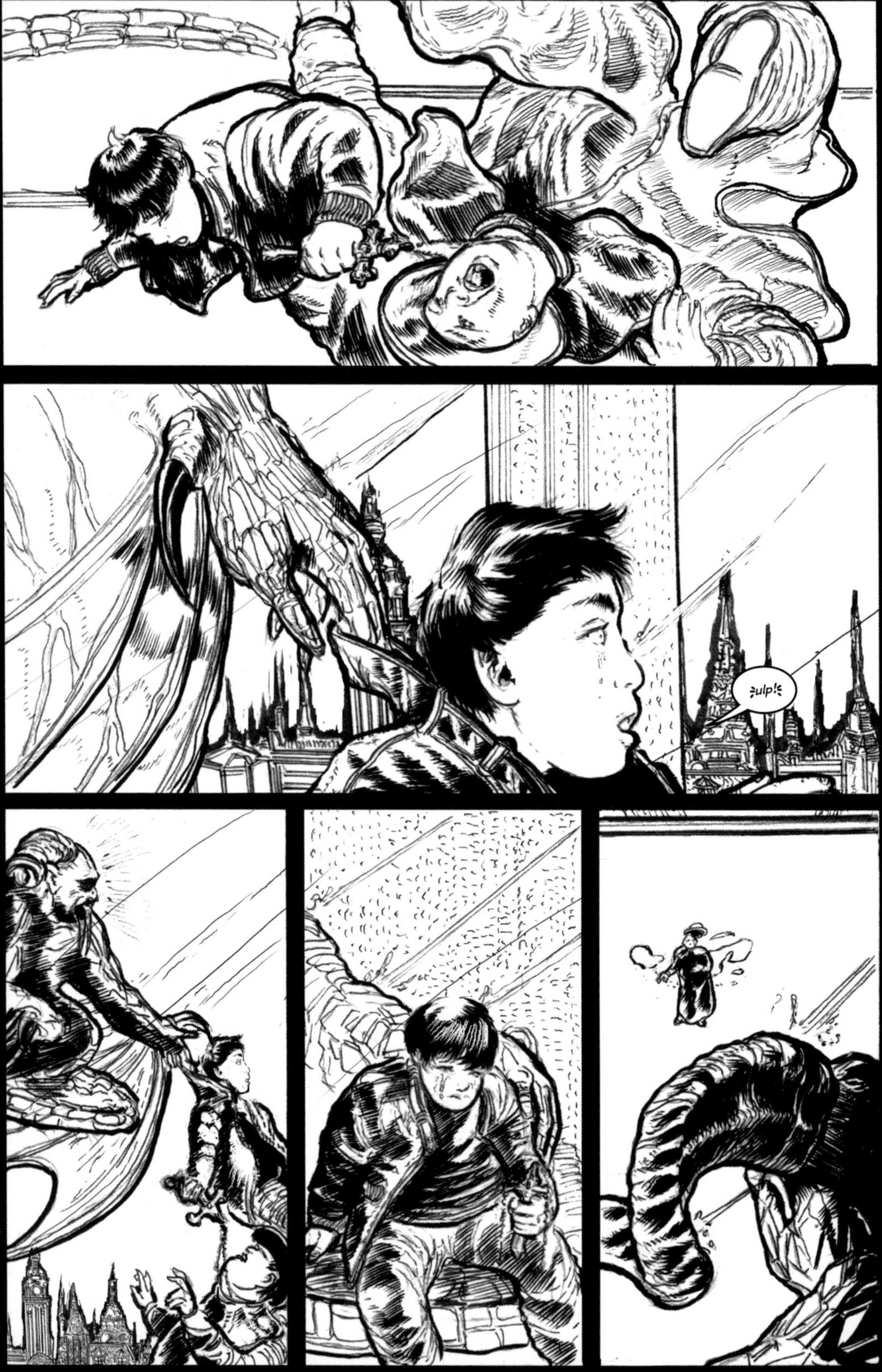
ulp!

Jane Yolen is the author of more than 350 books, including *Owl Moon*, *The Devil's Arithmetic*, and three graphic novels: *Foiled, Curses! Foiled Again*, and *The Last Dragon*. Her books and stories have won a Caldecott Medal, two Nebulas, and dozens of other awards. Six colleges and universities have given her honorary doctorates for her body of work. Also worthy of note: her Skylark Award—given by NESFA, the New England Science Fiction Association—set her good coat on fire. If you need to know more about her, visit her website at www.janeyolen.com

Adam Stemple is the author of fantasy novels and short stories including *Singer of Souls* and *Steward of Song*. Stemple and Jane Yolen have previously coauthored the Rock 'n' Roll Fairy Tale and Seelie Wars book series. Stemple also performs Celtic-influenced American folk rock. He is based in Minneapolis and online at adamstemple.com.

Orion Zangara is an illustrator and comic book artist who lives in Sterling, Virginia. He is a graduate of The Kubert School, an art trade school with a concentration in sequential art, founded by his grandfather Joe Kubert. Currently he is illustrating a soon-to-be-announced series for Image Comics. And he finds it very strange describing himself in the third person! You may reach him at www.orionzangara.com.